A Fair Deliverance

Brian Clegg

Copyright © 2021 Brian Clegg

www.brianclegg.net

The author has asserted his moral rights.

No part of this book may be reproduced in any form, or by any means, without prior permission in writing from the author.

All rights reserved.

ISBN-13: 9798727066638

DEDICATION

For Gillian, Rebecca and Chelsea

THE STEPHEN CAPEL MYSTERIES

1. A Lonely Height
2. A Timely Confession
3. A Spotless Rose
4. A Twisted Harmony
5. An End to Innocence
6. A Fall from Grace
7. A Fair Deliverance

ACKNOWLEDGMENTS

My thanks to historical fiction author Emma Darwin for details of the historical fiction world.

Marlborough does indeed have its Mop fairs, and a wonderful literary festival – but the festival and its organisers as portrayed here are entirely fictional and bear no resemblance to any real-world persons or events.

As with all the Capel books, I owe a huge debt to the brilliant authors of detective fiction who helped me fall in love with the genre, particularly Margery Allingham, P. D. James and Ruth Rendell.

CHAPTER 1

'Do we have to?' asked Stephen Capel. He pointed down the wide expanse of Marlborough's High Street, garishly lit by the primary-coloured bulbs of the fairground rides. Usually, the pretty market town's high street looked ridiculously wide – but with the fair in place it was clear this space had always been intended as a gathering place, rather than a through route.

'Look,' said Capel, 'there are burgers. Really greasy burgers, with fried onions. And proper plastic cheese. And barbecue sauce. Did I mention there were fried onions?'

'Don't be so feeble,' said Vicky. 'Margaret's going on the ride and she must be twice your age.'

The sturdy figure of Margaret LeVine was striding on ahead of them, acknowledging many of those she passed. 'Evening, Victor! Catherine, no children tonight? Hello, Jamie. I'll see you at the station on Monday. Nice to see you again, Nala. Suki – I need to speak to you later, it's quite urgent. Do you think that's wise, Dot?'

'It's like she's local royalty,' said Capel. 'In my job, I expect most people to know me in the village, but somewhere the size of Marlborough… it's remarkable.'

'Don't try to change the subject,' said Vicky. 'You can't get out of this by distracting me.'

'It's alright for you, but I hate fairground rides.'

'How can anyone not love a good ride? And this is

kids' stuff. Give me a proper rollercoaster any day. I'm going to drag you to Alton Towers or Blackpool before long.'

'That'd be cruel. I had a childhood trauma on a fairground ride that I've never recovered from.'

'Really?'

'When I was ten, my cousin Geena took me to a fair; she was always my favourite cousin. We went on the Waltzers. Geena was 16 and the fairground guys were buzzing around her like flies round a honeypot. So, our car got all the attention. I threw up all over Geena's best sundress, and she was not impressed, to say the least. It has made me feel unwell just to stand near a ride ever since. Even that metal-electric smell turns my stomach.'

'All the more reason to go for it and face your fear. Anyway, I'm no fan of fairground rides that spin you round like the Waltzers. You definitely don't have to go on them with me.'

'Erm, spinning actually,' said Capel, pointing at the ride in front of them. 'That thing is definitely spinning.'

'This is not at all like the Waltzers,' said Vicky. 'It's a completely different kind of motion.'

'How about I get the burgers while you go on the ride with Margaret? No need for you to queue, and I'll even pay for drinks.'

Vicky shook her head and pushed Capel to follow the rest of the queue as they shuffled towards the steps. 'You're getting on.'

The ride was a huge latticework, shaped like a cake tin without a lid – they climbed three steps and followed those in front to stand inside with their backs against the curved wall. Capel resisted the urge to reach for Vicky's hand and stood beside her. Margaret LeVine had positioned herself almost opposite them, her bob of short grey hair blending into the metalwork of the wall behind her. LeVine waved enthusiastically at Capel, who forced an unconvincing grin in reply.

'Don't look so worried,' whispered Vicky close to his ear. 'Just lie back and think of England.'

While Capel was still dredging his mind for a witty reply, a curved door slid shut across the entrance, completing the circle of the metal wall around them. An Elvis song blared out from the speakers over Capel's head. With a noisy jolt and a whiff of ozone, the ride began to rotate, rapidly picking up speed. Capel felt the metal wall behind him pressing into his back. Moments later he joined in a collective yelp as the floor dropped away, leaving them pinned against the wall by centrifugal force.

Capel reached for Vicky's hand as a teenager on the far side of the circle began to shuffle himself around until he was completely upside down. The shouts and squeals from the riders, blending with the roar of the music and the rumble of the mechanism, were so loud that for a moment Capel didn't notice the change in tone of the screams coming from the opposite side of the drum. An arc light was glaring into his eyes, making it difficult to see, but he could make out a girl, next to Margaret LeVine, her face distorted as she yelled. She seemed to be trying to reach out towards LeVine, but the force of the ride dragged her arms back. A blossom of red was spreading on LeVine's white top; something near the centre of the redness glinted as it tumbled away.

Capel worked himself up and sideways to get his

mouth as close as he could to Vicky's ear. 'Miss LeVine,' he yelled. 'Can you see?'

'Shit!' Vicky fought against the restraining force of the ride to get her phone out of her pocket and bring it to her ear.

'Stop this thing, someone's hurt!' Capel yelled, hoping to be heard by the operator, but the ride continued to spin.

'Shush!' said Vicky, elbowing Capel efficiently in the ribs. 'They can't hear you and I need to call this in.' With an effort, she pulled the hand with the phone away from the wall and to her ear. 'Police and ambulance… Marlborough High Street, the Mop Fair. There's been an incident on a ride… it's the – damn it, I can't remember what it's called – a big spinny thing where the floor drops away and you're pinned to the wall. Member of the public wounded – possible knife attack – looks serious. What? Detective Constable Vicky Denning, Avon and Somerset Police, based in Bath. I was just on the ride, nothing official. No, it's still going – no one on it can move… Yes, I will. Thanks.'

'Well?' asked Capel.

'With any luck they'll have officers on the scene by the time the ride stops. Look, I'm going to have to get to the entrance as soon as I'm able to move to prevent anyone on the ride from leaving the scene. As soon as it's possible, you need to get across to Margaret and see if you can do anything for her. Keep people away as much as you can. If it's a knife, make sure nobody pulls it out.'

'Okay,' shouted Capel.

It seemed an age before the spinning ride jerked a little and its mechanical roar started to drop in pitch.

The floor came up to meet them. Fighting the last of the force pinning her to the wall, Vicky levered herself away and loped over to the entrance, elbowing a confused-looking teen out of the way. Capel had forgotten that he had pushed himself up the wall and slid down to land heavily on the metal flooring. The other riders were starting to mill about – he worked his way around towards the slumped form of Margaret LeVine.

As the door opened, Vicky waved her hands, holding her warrant card. 'Police!' she shouted. 'Please stay on the ride for a few minutes longer. You are safe here, but we need to wait until other officers have arrived. No one leave until you have given your details.'

A blue flashing light flooded the ride from behind her, casting Vicky's indigo shadow in flickering relief across the baffled riders. Vicky turned as a pair of uniformed officers, a tubby bearded man and a tall woman, flanked her. 'DC Denning,' said Vicky. 'There's been an assault on the ride, possible stabbing. I've kept everyone on.'

'Thanks,' said the woman PC. 'We'll take it from here.' She waved at the ride operator. 'Turn that music off!' The song quit mid-syllable. The other officer shouted up to the riders: 'Please keep calm. Step down from the ride one at a time. We need to see some form of identification and to take your contact details. We'll get you off as soon as we can, but please bear with us. Please do not push.'

'Where's the victim?' the woman asked Vicky.

'Over the far side,' said Vicky. She pointed to the knot of people around where LeVine had fallen. 'I'll go and check on her.'

When Vicky had pushed her way through the small group, she found Capel, kneeling beside Margaret LeVine, holding her hand. Capel looked up as Vicky came into sight and shook his head. 'She's gone.' Someone behind him started sobbing.

'Okay, don't touch anything. We need to clear a bigger perimeter around the body. Can you move back, everyone, please? Who was next to her?'

The young woman that Capel had seen screaming, mascara streaked down her face, and a middle-aged man with a massive belly, a wispy purple beard and a tattered ACDC T-shirt raised their hands as if they were at school.

'I need to get your details,' said Vicky. 'They'll still want to find out more, so don't go anywhere, but if I can take down the basics and what you saw.' She pulled out her notebook and nodded at the man. 'You first, please.'

~

'Let's get this straight. You were on this ride at the Little Mop because you wanted to run a literary festival for your church in Bath?' Sergeant Crawford stared at Capel across the interview room table. The angle of the sergeant's eyebrows suggested she wasn't entirely convinced by his story.

'In Thornton Down to be precise, which is a village near Bath, but yes,' said Capel. 'I know it sounds a bit odd, but Margaret LeVine – the victim – has run Marlborough Literary Festival for years. She has a lot of experience and she offered to help me. Vicky – Detective Constable Denning – and I had come over to have a drink and a chat with Margaret, and she – Margaret, I mean – suggested that we came to the fair. She is… she was a big fan of the Mop. She even asked us if we'd come back again next week for the Big Mop.'

'Why Marlborough?' asked the sergeant. She ran a hand through her short hair. 'There must be plenty of other literary festivals out Bath way. I'm sure there are loads of arty types around there. It's a long way to come.'

'It wasn't that I thought of a festival and then found Margaret, but rather the other way round. She'd come out to Thornton Down, researching a book she was writing. A historical novel: that's what she wrote. We got to talking and I mentioned that we were looking for ways to raise church funds. It goes with the job. She told me that there'd been a really successful literary festival in a church north of Swindon – Kempsford, I think it was – and suggested I tried something similar, but on a smaller scale. As a result, Vicky and I came over to pick her brains.'

'And the pair of you were situated together on the other side of the ride to Miss LeVine?'

'That's right, pretty much diametrically opposite. Once the ride was going, it was impossible to move around, apart from shuffling a little. I saw one boy manage to turn upside down, but that seemed to be about the limit of movement. And it was extremely difficult to lift your arms much away from the sides. Only the people either side of her had a chance to do anything, but even for them, lifting a knife far enough to stab her would have been near-impossible. I didn't see it happen. She was already bleeding when I noticed that something was wrong.'

'So, you believe that there was a knife involved?'

'It's a guess. I thought she'd been stabbed. I assumed...'

'Did you find a knife?'

'No, when I got over to her after the ride had stopped there was nothing I could see in the wound and I applied pressure to try to reduce blood loss. I thought I saw something shiny drop away from her when the ride was still running, but I didn't find anything that it could have been on the floor. Of course, it might just have been blood that caught the light. There was a floodlight shining in my eye, so it was difficult to see clearly. And the floor sort of dropped away during the ride, so if anything had fallen from the wound, it would have gone over the edge. I presume people are checking underneath.'

'Oh, yes, they are,' said the sergeant. 'Don't worry about that. And what happened when you first got there? To Miss LeVine. Did she say anything to you?'

'She was dead,' said Capel. 'I did what I could, but she was already dead.'

~

Capel had to wait around for an hour before Vicky turned up. The surprisingly large police station on George Lane in Marlborough looked more like a nondescript two storey modern office block, were it not for the blue lamp and sign outside. The station was always going to be quite busy on a Mop Fair evening, dealing with the usual minor incidents that accompany any lively public gathering, but tonight it was heaving with the riders and witnesses who had been standing near the ride.

'We can go,' Vicky said as she came out of an

office to the small waiting area, where Capel was sat on the floor as there were five times as many people as there were seats. 'Sorry I took so long. They needed some help with the basic processing. They're not used to dealing with these kinds of numbers.'

'I'm sure they were grateful to have a professional on the scene when it happened – assuming they don't suspect you. I got the impression they were a bit dubious about me.'

'It's not surprising. Just because you – we – were the only ones on the ride who they know had any connection to Margaret. It's relatively rare that an attack like this is totally random, unless it's terrorist related or due to a mental health issue. There were no indications that's the case here. And there were far easier opportunities to stab someone out on the street if it was just a random assault. But they know it wasn't us who stabbed her – the laws of physics pretty much make that impossible.'

'I wonder how often physics is an alibi?' said Capel. 'Sorry, that sounded thoughtless. It's such a shock. Let's get home: I don't know about you, but I could do with something more substantial than candy floss and a fizzy drink.'

CHAPTER 2

Capel's phone woke him up the next morning. He peered blearily at the time as he answered it. Seven thirty. As a vicar, particularly a vicar who was engaged to a police officer, he was used to early calls, but was never going to be a natural early riser. 'Er, yes, hello? Stephen Capel.'

'Did I wake you?' the female voice on the other end of the line was familiar, but Capel's brain was not yet engaged enough yet to be able to place her.

'Possibly,' said Capel. 'Sorry, I'm not very with it.'

'Ah. Its Chief Inspector Morley. Is Denning there? She's not answering her phone.'

'Sorry, no, she's at her mother's flat at the moment. The phone reception there is terrible. Her mum heard there'd been trouble in Marlborough on the news – she knew we were over there last night, and Vicky felt she ought to call in and reassure her. You know her mother moved up to Claverton from Dorset, so she could be nearer to her? Vicky ended up staying the night at the flat.'

'Okay. I need to speak to Denning as soon as I can. Wiltshire Police have asked if they can borrow her for a few weeks. Their Marlborough station doesn't have enough staff for a major incident, and they're aware of the Bath connection after, erm, Miss LeVine came over to see you. They thought Denning could follow up at your end and give them a few hours in Marlborough. I say "a few hours", but experience suggests it's more likely to be a few weeks.'

'You're happy with that?' asked Capel. 'Vicky said

you're short of staff as it is.'

'We never have enough officers,' said Morley. 'But it doesn't do any harm to get yourself into a neighbouring force's good books. You don't know when you'll need a favour in return.'

'Fair enough. No worries, I'll get her to call you as soon as I can.'

Capel pulled on his dressing gown, shuffled down the stairs and switched on the coffee machine. As it hissed and rattled, he called Vicky's mother's landline.

Vicky answered. 'Do you know what time it is?' She didn't sound impressed.

'Tell that to your boss. She rang me five minutes ago. I was asleep at the time.'

'So you thought that you'd share the pain around?'

'Absolutely. Also, she wants to speak to you ASAP. Apparently, the Wiltshire police were so impressed with you that they want to borrow you to help work on Margaret LeVine's case.'

'Terrific,' said Vicky. She didn't sound happy.

'I thought you'd be pleased. A chance to catch Margaret's killer.'

'Yes, of course, I'd love to help put whatever bastard did it away. But I know what the locals can be like when they get someone sent in from outside their patch. I mean, we're all supposed to be in this together, but they don't exactly welcome you with open arms. I'll ring Morley. As it happens it's been quiet in Bath of late, so…'

'Hang on, there's someone at the door. Does no one understand the concept of Sunday morning lie-ins? I might as well have not bothered wheedling Alan Rhees into taking the 8.30 for me.'

'At least they're bothering you on the day when

you actually work, rather than the rest of the week.'

'Ha ha. Bog off and call the chief inspector so she can order you around, detective constable. I'll see you this afternoon.'

Capel disconnected the call and hurried to the door as the bell rang again. He opened it to see a tall, thin man in his thirties. His brown hair was cut very short, little more than stubble. He was wearing a brown suit without a tie. Great, thought Capel, all I need at this time of the morning is a door-to-door salesman.

'Is it the Reverend Capel?' the man asked, pronouncing the name as 'capple'.

'Yes,' said Capel. 'Well, the Reverend Capel, to be precise.' He stressed 'cay-pull.'

'Sorry, I've only ever seen your name written down. My name is Russell Levine. And while we're being precise about surnames, it's spelled without a capital V in the middle. That was a literary affectation of my aunt's.'

'You're Margaret LeVine's nephew? I am very sorry for your loss. It must have come as a great shock.'

'We were close. My parents are both dead, and Aunt Margaret didn't have any children of her own.' Levine seemed to notice Capel's dressing gown for the first time. 'Look, I'm sorry, I suppose I thought all vicars were up at the crack of dawn on a Sunday. I didn't mean to drag you out of bed, but I wanted to catch you before you had to go to the church. I can come back later if it'd be more convenient.'

'No, that's fine, honestly. I was already up, and I don't have a service until 10.30. I've put the coffee on – would you like one?'

'That would be extremely acceptable, thank you.'

Capel led the way into the kitchen and pointed Levine to the kitchen table. 'Take a seat. Would you like some toast as well?'

'I must admit, I haven't had any breakfast.'

'That's settled then.' Capel pushed bread into the toaster and assembled the paraphernalia of breakfast. 'How did you hear about your aunt's death, if you don't mind me asking?'

'It was all over the news. TV and online.'

'The police haven't contacted you yet?'

Levine frowned. 'Yes, of course they have, but I had already seen it on the news. I was in shock. I suppose it took them a little while to track me down. I'm her next of kin, but I don't know how they were supposed to know that.'

'I can see it would be difficult.' Capel lined up the toast in the rack that Vicky's mum had given him for his birthday and put it in the centre of the table. 'Help yourself – there's butter there and jam or marmalade. So, what exactly can I do for you?'

'I know Aunt Margaret came to see you a couple of times recently. I wondered if you could tell me anything about that, under the circumstances. I'm trying to understand all this.'

'Okay,' said Capel. It seemed surprising Levine hadn't asked about the previous evening's events, but perhaps he didn't know that Capel had been there when Miss LeVine had died, or perhaps her death was still too raw. 'As you'll know better than me, Margaret wrote historical fiction for a living. She was researching a new book set in this area in Anglo-Saxon times. It seems that Thornton Down was an Anglo-Saxon settlement. Apparently, it was originally just called Down, but in medieval times they added the "Thornton" part after some long-forgotten bigwigs. Local lords of the manor, that kind of thing. Margaret's new book was set in Down and the surrounding area.'

'And you provided her with some local colour?'

'Not a lot, no. She had hoped that there would be old records or memorials in the church, but it's a relatively modern building – mid-Victorian – and though there had been a Norman church on the site, everything from the earlier establishment was lost in a fire, some time in the seventeen hundreds. We've got nothing even close to any Anglo-Saxon relics. So, after the initial disappointment, it was more a case of her helping me than the other way round.'

'I don't understand. In what way was she helping you?'

'As you're probably aware, churches are always pretty short of funds.' Capel smiled and ran a hand through his hair. 'Church buildings are beautiful, but not cheap to run. And these days we're also pretty focused on finding ways to help parishioners to reconnect with their local church when the majority of them are no longer regular churchgoers. Margaret mentioned to me her involvement with the Marlborough Literary Festival, and she was giving me tips on how we might put together our own little festival here.'

'Oh, yes,' said Levine. 'She was always fond of telling people what to do.' He frowned. 'I didn't mean that the way it sounded. She was kind. Good at helping people.'

'Hmm, yes,' said Capel. 'She was very thoughtful.'

'I'm sure. So, she didn't say anything at all about

the detail of her new book? Any locations around here that she intended to use, or any significant plot points she had in mind?'

'Not really,' said Capel. 'Is there something important that I'm missing? Is this connected to her death in some way? You know we were there last night when she died? And my fiancée, who was with me, is…'

'What? No, it's not about that at all. I'm not playing detective, I think we're best leaving all that to the police. It just felt like there was something missing in what I know.' Levine polished off his slice of toast and stood up. 'I really shouldn't take up any more of your time.' Standing, he took a last drink of his coffee and smiled. 'That was very good of you, thanks. I'm sorry to have troubled you – I really ought to be on my way. Thank you so much for sparing me the time.'

'You are welcome,' said Capel. He opened a kitchen drawer and rifled through it, pulling out a business card. 'Look, my number's on here. If there's anything you want to talk about, any help you need with arranging the funeral or whatever, let me know. And as I was going to say, my fiancée is a police officer. She's actually working on your aunt's case – so if you need to get in touch with the police side of things, I can easily pass a message on through her.'

Levine's eyes widened. 'Is she, really? That's so kind.' His smile had become very taut. 'I'm afraid I must be off now. I've taken up far too much of your time.'

Capel saw Levine out and headed back to the kitchen to finish his breakfast. He had just spread a second slice of toast with thick-cut marmalade when the doorbell rang again.

'What is this, rush hour? It's like Piccadilly Circus,' Capel muttered to himself as he tightened the belt of his dressing gown and headed for the door. Perhaps Levine had forgotten something. But he could tell even before he opened the door that it was not his earlier visitor who was waiting outside. The person the other side behind the frosted glass was shorter and considerably less skinny.

When Capel opened the door, he thought for a moment he recognised the man who stood waiting, but realised that it was because his new visitor had a passing resemblance to the actor David Mitchell, with watery eyes, floppy hair and a dark beard. He seemed distracted, frown lines creasing his forehead. Rather than looking directly at Capel, the focus of his gaze seemed to be somewhere in the corridor behind.

'Good morning,' said Capel. 'Can I help you?'

'I hope so,' said the man. 'My name is Russell Levine. I'm Margaret LeVine's nephew.'

CHAPTER 3

FOUR WEEKS EARLIER

Margaret LeVine sat in Capel's dubious looking second-best armchair, sipping from the mug of tea he had given her.

'Have you ever read the Anglo-Saxon Chronicle, Mr Capel?' She punctuated her words with the chocolate finger he had offered her.

Capel fought back the urge to say that he usually read the Guardian. 'Er, just Capel is fine. No, I can't say that I have read it.'

'You should, it's fascinating.' LeVine dug into her large leather handbag and pulled out a battered brown hardback that appeared to have long lost its dustcover. 'It was the key starting point for my next book. Bath features in the Chronicle a number of times, as you might imagine for a city that has such a long history. Let me give you an example.'

Capel opened his mouth to speak, but decided it was pointless to interrupt and sat back with his coffee, picking up a biscuit.

'Erm, right. This is the year 973. Or 972 or 974 – as you are no doubt well aware, there are four main copies of the Chronicle and they don't always agree on chronology. Sometimes the differences are stark. Here we are: "In this year Edgar, ruler of the English, with a great company, was consecrated king in the ancient borough Acemannescaeaster." What do you think of that?'

'Erm, yes,' said Capel. He felt as if he was back at school, being asked a difficult question by the teacher. About a lesson where he hadn't paid attention. 'I don't really, er…'

'Edgar, as I'm sure you will realise, would become known as Edgar the Peaceful as a result of the relative stability of his reign. However, that word "relative" is the key one here: these were still extremely difficult times. Edgar became king of England way back in 959 when he was still a teenager, but he wasn't crowned until he was getting on for thirty. He died only a couple of years after the coronation. They say that the ceremony devised for him formed the kernel of what has been the English coronation ceremony ever since, right through to our present monarch.'

'That's fascinating, but where does Bath come in?'

'Ah, yes, I ought to give you the context. Hang on, blah, blah… "consecrated king in the ancient borough Acemannescaeaster - the men who dwell in this island also call it by another name, Bath. There great joy had come to all on that blessed day which the children of men call and name the day of Pentecost. There was assembled a crowd of priests, a great throng of learned monks, as I have heard tell." Wonderful, isn't it? You can really feel the writer's enthusiasm. It feels so genuine.'

'Indeed,' said Capel. 'I see the connection now with Bath, of course. I hadn't heard of, erm, Ace Man… that other name. So, you're writing a book that's set here in Edgar's time?'

'No, no, that was just an example that I rather enjoy as a way to give a feel for the chroniclers in action. We need to go back a few years to 905 or 906 for the setting of my novel.' LeVine flicked backward through a few pages of the Chronicle. 'Here we are. "In this year Alfred, who was reeve at Bath, died. And that same year the peace was established at Tiddingfield, just as King Edward decreed, both with the East Angles and Northumbrians." That's Edward the Elder, you understand, King of the Anglo Saxons, Alfred the Great's son. But my book concerns Alfred *the reeve* and the circumstances of his death. Too much historical fiction is concerned with the doings of royalty, don't you think?'

'What exactly was a reeve?' asked Capel, not wanting to get into a discussion about historical fiction, which on his few attempts he had found too florid to be readable.

'The reeve was an extremely important figure in the community. The Normans downgraded the title, but in Anglo-Saxon times, a reeve was the local representative of the Crown. At the shire level, you had the post of shire reeve, a title that would become contracted to be the more familiar "sheriff" – he was the senior law officer for the county. But in a location as important as Bath, bearing in mind that Edgar the Peaceful would be crowned there only a few decades later, the *city* reeve would also be an extremely important person – this Alfred was the first ever reeve mentioned for Bath, and one who is said to have been extremely rich.'

'But the Chronicle doesn't tell us much about his life?'

'Only what I read out to you. However, there are plenty of local myths and legends – and, to be honest, if you are putting together a piece of historical fiction as I am, it can help not to be too tied down by pesky documentation. The looser the facts, the more literary freedom the author is given without the hist fic police descending on you like wolves on the fold.' She sighed. 'I sometimes wish I was writing fifty years ago – back then, they could get away with murder. Now you practically have to give references. It's supposed to be a story, for God's sake.' She paused for a sip of tea. 'Sorry, got astride my hobbyhorse. Excellent tea, by the way: thank you. Now, speaking of the literati such as my distinguished colleagues in the world of historical fiction, about your idea for a literary festival…'

~

PRESENT DAY

'Erm, ah,' said Capel, looking doubtfully at his second visitor of the morning.

'Is it an inconvenient time?' The bearded man at the door, the second to claim to be Margaret LeVine's nephew, eyed Capel's dressing gown cautiously.

'No, it's not that,' said Capel. 'I'll go into why I need it in a moment, but do you have any form of photo ID?'

The man frowned. 'Yes, I think so.' He dragged a large leather wallet from his back pocket and rifled through it, pulling out a driving licence, which he handed over to Capel. The photograph was certainly his – and it identified him as Russell Levine.

'Thank you,' said Capel, handing it back. 'Can I get you a tea or coffee? Then I can explain why I asked that.'

Levine shrugged. 'Okay, fine. Coffee, black with nothing added.'

Capel led the way into kitchen and poured another

coffee. It was a good job he'd made a large pot. 'About half an hour ago I had an unexpected visitor. He said his name was Russell Levine and that he was Margaret's nephew. I gave him my condolences, which should have gone to you it seems, and he asked me why your aunt had been in touch with me, which now I think of it seems distinctly odd under the circumstances.'

'God,' said Levine. 'Really? Someone pretending to be me? That's weird. You ought to tell the police.'

'I will,' said Capel. 'My fiancée is a police detective – she's working on the case, in fact. I'll make sure that they keep an eye out for this fake version of you. I'm sorry I was taken in – but he was entirely plausible. I had no reason to suspect that he wasn't who he said he was. He started by saying how he spelled his surname without the capital V.'

'That's true,' said Levine, 'I do. He must have known something about me. The family name is Levine like mine, but my aunt thought it would look more interesting as a historical novelist to put in the second capital letter. If I'm honest, I always thought it was a mistake. A touch pretentious.'

'If it worked for her,' said Capel, 'then why not. She was a lovely lady. What is it I can do for you?'

'I don't know, really.' Levine bit his top lip. 'I suppose I hoped you could explain to me how it all happened. How she died. I know you were meeting up with Aunt Margaret at the Mop Fair last night: she'd mentioned it to me.'

'I really don't know that I can tell you any more than the police will have already done.'

'That was very little indeed.'

'Margaret was meeting up with us – my fiancée

Vicky was there too – we'd arranged to see her to discuss a literary festival that I am hoping to start here. Well, I was hoping to, though I won't be going ahead with it now. But we really hadn't spoken much at that point. It was Margaret's idea to go on a few rides at the Mop Fair first, before we went for a drink and a chat. She seemed to love the whole fairground thing. We were on the ride – I was on one side of it with Vicky, and Margaret was opposite us. I didn't see what happened. One moment she was fine, the next…'

'I'm sorry, it must be unpleasant for you, remembering it.'

'It is hard. I hadn't known her long, but Margaret was a wonderful character.'

'Yes. How exactly did she know you?'

'Sorry, I'm getting confused between what I've told the other you and the real you, if you see what I mean. Margaret contacted me first, asking about local records and some locations for a book she was writing. It was going to be set in the tenth century in Bath and around these parts. Vicars are often a good source of local history information, apparently, though to be honest I wasn't able to help her much.'

'That sounds like Aunt Margaret. She liked to immerse herself in a locale when she was writing a book. She always said that a sense of place was the key to good historical fiction. That the story had to be embedded in the landscape, and you could still get a feel for the location's historical context, particularly in villages away from towns and cities. Societies come and go, she said, but the landscape remains, and we can still absorb a sense of how it shaped the past. I think that might be why she was up for next year's

Walter Scott Prize. She still is, I suppose. I don't honestly know if it can be awarded posthumously.'

'I'm sorry, I don't know what the Walter Scott Prize is.'

'I suppose you'd call it the Historical Fiction equivalent of the Booker Prize. She'd already won the HWA Gold Award, but the Walter Scott is the absolute pinnacle in her field.'

'It would have been well-deserved, I'm sure. If I'm honest, I haven't read any of her books, though Vicky bought me one, set in Henry VIII's time – I've been meaning to start it this week.'

'That would be *The Rose and the Thorn*. Yes, that's the novel that's up for the Walter Scott. She wasn't a hack writer, you know, she was the sort of historical fiction author who was quite capable of being nominated for the big name literary prizes too. And she managed her writing commitments despite putting all that time and effort into the Marlborough Festival.'

Capel glanced at the clock. 'Look, I'm really sorry – someone stood in for me on my early duties this morning, but I am going to have to prepare for the 10:30 service. Are you in these parts for long? Perhaps we could meet up again when there's more time?'

'That would be wonderful,' said Levine. 'If it's not too much trouble, I would love it if you could show me where my aunt had intended to visit with you, but never managed to. This sense of place thing has got to me, I think. I'd like to know what it was that inspired her. I have to go up to London today, but I could come back down here on Tuesday if that would work for you.'

'Of course,' said Capel. 'We could meet for lunch, perhaps, and I can take you to the places Margaret and I had discussed.'

As he showed Levine out, Capel was already trying to get his mind back into the familiar Sunday morning mode, the calm preparation for taking a service. It was not easy.

~

Vicky turned up late in the evening. Capel had been watching a Sunday night murder mystery on the TV, but he had lost track halfway through and was drifting in and out of sleep. As the front door banged, he jerked upright and checked his watch. It was coming up to ten.

'Sorry I'm so late,' said Vicky as she came in. 'Everything takes longer when you're off home territory.'

'It's not a problem,' said Capel. 'Can I get you a drink?'

Vicky shook her head. 'I just want to get to bed. How do you fancy a trip out to sunny Swindon tomorrow? Apparently, it's the nearest mortuary space they could get to Marlborough. They took Margaret's body there.'

'You mean go to the mortuary for the autopsy? It's not really my thing.'

'No, don't worry, not for that. But the pathologist wants to speak to me, and I'd like you to come along as you were there when it happened.'

'It'll make a change from dealing with Roland the Ripper, I suppose.'

'Ah,' said Vicky.

'What do you mean, ah? Surely your beloved godfather can't work for Wiltshire as well as Avon and Somerset?'

'No, but there's apparently a shortage of forensic pathologists at the moment, so he's helping out over there until they can get someone else in charge, and because I'm involved…'

'They thought they'd bring Roland in for this one. I call that nepotism.'

'You know you love him, really. At least he's a known quantity.'

'I suppose. What time is he expecting you?'

'Nine AM, bright and early, at the Great Western Hospital.'

'Wouldn't miss it for the world. But in the meantime, I've got some interesting news for you. Margaret's nephew came to see me earlier. Twice.'

'Anything interesting to say?'

'Oh, yes. Both times.'

'There's obviously something you're dying to tell me.'

'Let's say he was a changed man.'

CHAPTER 4

The mortuary at the Swindon hospital was in the basement, tucked discretely away from those who weren't looking for it. Capel followed Vicky through a featureless door into a large office.

'Ah, Capel, good to see you again. It's time we had another pint.' Dr Roland Mclean stripped off a pair of latex gloves and dropped them into a pedal bin. He bounced into a chair in front of an empty desk, folded his hands across his stomach and smiled benignly.

'That would be enjoyable,' said Capel, taking one of the seats opposite. 'I gather you've got news for Vicky.'

'I think that's my line,' said Vicky. 'What have you got for us, Roland?'

'I'll be honest,' said Mclean, 'I was inclined to curse you for being responsible for dragging me over here, but I'm really glad now that you got me involved. It's a cracker, it really is.'

Capel winced.

'All we know is that the victim had an injury with significant bleeding, presumed to be a stab wound, but that there was no knife when we got to her.' Vicky paged through her notebook. 'I can also confirm that no weapon was found under the ride and no one appeared to pull one from the wound. Down below the ride floor there was just the usual fairground crap, plus loads of those novelty pencils they were giving out to advertise the literary festival earlier in the day. You'd think the kids would have held onto them.'

'I blame Happy Meals,' said Capel. 'Even a nice pencil was special once, but when you get something fancy with every cheap meal it devalues…'

'Aye,' Mclean cut in, attempting a Yorkshire accent. 'When I were a lad, we were lucky to have a piece of coal to play with. And we had to share that between nine of us.'

Vicky coughed. 'Several of the pencils found below where Miss LeVine was when the ride stopped had blood on them, but it's likely that it dripped down. There was considerable blood loss. You've been sent all the evidence to be examined, I believe.'

'Are you saying that she was stabbed with a pencil?' said Capel.

'Hardly,' said Mclean. He opened a drawer and pulled out a bright red pencil. It had four green feathers fixed to one end; Mclean waved it around as if it were a magic wand. 'This isn't one of the ones with blood on, and it's clear of prints and DNA.' He tossed it to Capel. 'As you can see, the pencil is blunt – it has not been sharpened. There's no point on it to make a wound, even if it had been strong enough to penetrate clothing and flesh, which it clearly isn't. And the other end's hopeless as a weapon with the fluffy decorations stuck to it. Keep it, I've got plenty more.'

Capel's eyes narrowed, but he didn't speak.

'So,' said Mclean, 'on to the good stuff. Our Miss LeVine was penetrated by a sharp object, flattish, about a centimetre across in the wide direction, to use non-technical terms that you can understand – it pierced her heart. But what that object was, I have no idea.'

'She wasn't shot?' asked Capel.

'Would that even be possible?' asked McLean. 'I got the impression that the centrifugal force was so strong that no one on the ride could have aimed a gun while they were spinning around. And the ride had high metal walls, so a shot couldn't have come from the street level.'

'There was the operator,' said Capel. 'He had a clear view into the ride from that sort of observing pod he was in. And the whole thing was open at the top. Someone could have shot her from an upstairs window, over one of the shops in the high street. No one ever takes notice of the upstairs windows in a high street - you only see the shops – but they've all got them.'

'I don't think it could have been the operator,' said Vicky. 'He has been eliminated because he was on CCTV all the time. Apparently, they've had trouble with staff misbehaving in the past and they're recorded. You'd certainly have to be a damned good shot to hit a fast-moving target like that, though I suppose it can't be ruled out. We will need to check if anyone had access to any upstairs windows with a direct line of fire.'

'Of course, your Miss LeVine might not have been a specific target,' said Mclean. 'The killer could simply have wanted to kill anyone on the ride. As you're aware, terror incidents are something we have to allow for in such circumstances. But the discussion is irrelevant as she wasn't shot. There was no bullet. We've got an entry wound with no accompanying exit wound. Bullets don't just fall out if they fail to pass straight through a body. And even if one could, there wasn't a bullet on the ground.'

'Ooh, ooh,' said Capel. 'What if it was an ice bullet?'

Mclean groaned. 'First of all, an ice bullet would almost certainly have been destroyed when the gun was fired, destroyed by the force of the explosive charge. The shock waves would shatter it. But even it hadn't been, it would not be hard enough to survive hitting someone at the speed a bullet flies. You know they can easily travel at over 1,000 miles per hour – faster than the speed of sound. At that rate, ice would have fragmented on impact. And even if it could have penetrated, I doubt it if it would have melted entirely before you got to the scene, and we would have been left with some kind of watery remnant.'

'What about frozen blood?' said Capel. 'If they got hold of Margaret's blood, that would presumably be undetectable.'

Mclean shook his head and looked over at Vicky. 'You've been letting him watch Silent Witness again, haven't you Vic? No. Leaving aside the fact that we're not certain that Miss LeVine was the intended target, a blood bullet would shatter rather than penetrate just as much as would pure water ice. Apart from anything else, this isn't a bullet entry wound. It's entirely the wrong shape – more like a bladed object. Though the force profile… that is unusual for a blade, I'll say that.'

'You could have said that it wasn't any kind of bullet to begin with,' said Capel.

'I was enjoying your venture into wild speculation far too much.'

'Come on, boys,' said Vicky, 'play nicely. Is there anything else you can tell us, Roland?'

Mclean frowned. 'I'll be honest, there's very little. We'll keep looking. But I don't think you're going to get an answer any time soon.'

~

Vicky drove them down from the hospital to the police station in Marlborough. Capel was unusually quiet, rolling the pencil Mclean had given him between his fingers.

'What's the matter?' Vicky asked as she pulled into the car park.

'I'm not sure, really. It's frustrating, I suppose, not knowing how it was done.'

'Well, maybe if we can find out who your fake Russell really was it will help us with the who did it, and that'll get us to the how.'

'Yes, maybe,' said Capel. 'If I'm honest, I'm dreading doing this.'

'What, the E-FIT? It's not painful, you know.'

'I know, but I'm hopeless at describing faces. I mean, he had very short brownish hair, greying a bit… I'm not even sure what colour his eyes were. I doubt I could even describe you well enough for the picture to be recognisable.'

'You'll do fine,' said Vicky. 'Your nephew impersonator is probably the best lead we've got at the moment.' She dropped Capel off in an office and headed across to the incident room. She hesitated outside the door. The locals had been friendly enough at a superficial level, but she was still being treated as an outsider.

'It won't open itself.'

Vicky turned quickly to see the local Inspector, Bill

Davis, waiting behind her.

'Sorry, sir.'

'Don't worry, you're just in time for a briefing.' Davis nodded at the door. 'Go on, then.'

'Sorry,' Vicky said again and walked in. Lacking a separate meeting room, the team had dragged a couple of desks to one side, so they could sit in a U-shape, facing an array of whiteboards. Vicky recognised the sergeant – Sergeant Crawford, but she couldn't remember her first name – and a pair of detective constables, but there were five other staff in the room she couldn't place.

'Right then,' said Davis, rubbing his hands together, 'where shall we start? Perhaps our temporary recruit DC Denning could fill us in with what she discovered from our equally imported pathologist? Despite the rumours, there is not a takeover bid taking place. There are no plans for the Avon and Somerset force to merge with Wiltshire Constabulary.'

The laugh he got from the others was half-hearted at best, and Sergeant Crawford rolled her eyes at Vicky. 'It's only a matter of time,' said Vicky. She quickly filled them in with Roland's thoughts on the weapon and the possible visibility of the ride from upper windows along the street.

'Okay,' said Davis, 'We'll need someone to check with all the premises with windows overlooking the ride. Denning, you can do that, since you came up with the bright idea. Crawford, what have we got on LeVine so far?'

The sergeant flicked her finger a couple of times across the iPad in front of her. 'Widow, aged sixty-eight. Lived alone – the only relative we know of is her nephew, Russell Levine (no capital V). He's a part time restauranteur, part time poet. You know the sort.'

'And that means what, exactly, Alicia?'

Crawford grimaced. 'You know, arty farty, minor public school type. As far as we know, Miss LeVine didn't seem to have any close friends, but a number of associates she was in regular contact with, mostly either from professional, literary or historical circles.' Crawford passed around a printed list. 'Here we go. There's the other members of the festival committee, her publisher – she seems mainly to have dealt with this Maneet Patel, an editor there – and the historical fiction trade seems to be quite a close-knit community. I mean, she was no Hilary Mantel, but she had a few close contacts amongst the second rank authors. Apparently, she had something of a… feud with this, erm, Cherie Taylor. Wrote the same kind of books, rivals for awards and all that kind of thing.'

Davis grunted. 'Bloody literary types, definition of a storm in a teacup, if you ask me. Share out the interviews, Alicia. You, Denning, you can have our author.'

'Thank you, sir,' said Vicky. 'There's something you should know. My fiancé, Stephen Capel…'

'The god botherer,' said Davis to a snigger from the others.

'Yes,' said Vicky. 'He had a visit yesterday morning from the nephew, Russell Levine. Twice.'

'That's eager,' said Crawford.

'Not so much eager as weird,' said Vicky. 'Two separate people came to see him, both of them claiming to be Russell Levine.'

Davis jerked upright in his chair. 'Now that is

interesting. Have you got a statement from Mr, erm…' he glanced down at his iPad. 'Mr Capel?'

'Yes,' said Vicky. 'It's on the system already. The first Russell seems to have been the imposter – the second one, Capel checked his ID. He had no reason initially to suspect that the first visitor was anyone other than who he said he was. The fake Russell was trying to get information out of Capel on Miss LeVine's research for her next book. She visited Capel about four weeks ago and he seemed far more interested in that than her death.'

'And we have no idea who this man was?'

'No, not yet,' said Vicky. 'I asked Capel to come in to do an E-FIT. He's here now.'

'Let's crack on with this, then,' said Davis. 'The boss is expecting results fast on this one. The powers that be have to decide whether or not to let the Big Mop go ahead next Saturday. My inclination is to cancel it if we've got a nutter at large.' He frowned. 'Crawford, where's DC Sutton? I had him down to do the E-FIT.'

'He had to follow up a lead, sir. Dean can do it.'

'Fair enough. What are we waiting for, people?'

~

Vicky checked off the Castle and Ball pub in her notebook and moved onto the last of the premises that had a chance of having line-of-site view to the ride from an upper room, a shop called Blatant that seemed to be part gift shop, part perfume store. She held her warrant card up to the young woman behind the counter. 'Hello, I'm Detective Constable Denning. I am making enquiries about the incident on the High Street on Saturday night.'

'Oh, that was terrible.'

'You are?'

'Kara. Kara Christiensen.'

'Could you spell that?'

'Kara with a K and it's C H R I S T I E N S E N. My dad's Danish.'

'Were you working on Saturday?'

'Yes, we were open late – we always do for the Mops. Not that there were many people in at any one time, but business was quite steady.'

'Would it be possible to take a look at the upper floors?'

'Of course. Hang on.' The shop assistant turned and shouted to the back of the shop: 'Raul, can you come on the till, please.' She turned back to Vicky. 'Do you want to follow me?'

They headed up the stairs to the first floor perfume shop. It was impossible to get near two of the windows where tall shelving units stood in the way, but the third was easily accessible. 'Do these windows open?'

'Yes, we sometimes open them in the summer. It gets really hot in here.'

Vicky nodded. She looked across to the ride where the death had happened, cordoned off with blue and white tape. Although she could see into the top of the ride, the angle was too shallow to have a direct line of sight to the riders. 'What about the next floor up?'

'It's a stockroom. It's locked when we're open. Only staff have access to it.'

'How many of you were on shift that night?'

'Just me. We're not supposed to be in on our own in the evening, but the other guy called in at the last minute, and I really don't mind.'

'Can we go up?'

'Sure.' Christiensen led the way up a narrow staircase signposted 'Staff only' and unlocked a door at the top. The stock room was dingy, a contrast to the elegant, minimalist fittings of the rest of the building. It looked as if it had originally been divided into a pair of bedrooms. Part of the partition had been removed, with a piece of faded yellow wallpaper hanging loose from the edge. The floor was dirty, with what looked like mouse droppings in the corner.

'Not so smart up here,' said Vicky.

'Yeah, we keep meaning to clear it up, but… you know how it is. There's never time.'

Vicky squeezed past a pile of boxes to the window, which she slid open, letting in a cold blast of air. From here there was a perfect line of sight to the inside of the ride, as there had been from several of the top floor windows in other buildings. 'Did you come up to this floor yourself on Saturday night?'

'What? No. Even if I'd wanted to, I couldn't have left the till alone without shutting the place up. There's CCTV so I can see the first floor there too. No, the only one who came up here was one of your lot.'

'Sorry? One of my lot?'

'Police – you know, when you were doing the security check.'

'Did you get a name for the officer?'

'No. It was a youngish guy, but… no, sorry.'

'That's fine,' said Vicky. 'Could I look at the CCTV from Saturday night?'

'Sorry, it doesn't record. It's just so someone on the till can make sure everything's okay on the first floor.'

'Never mind. I won't take up any more of your time right now, but we may have to come back and ask a couple more questions.'

As Vicky left the shop, her mobile rang. 'DC Denning.'

'Hi, it's Sergeant Crawford.'

'Hi, Sarge.'

'Call me Alicia – we're not that kind of outfit. Just stick to boss or guv with Inspector Davis. How've you got on with the upper floor windows?'

Vicky sighed. 'Nothing stands out. There are…' she took a look at her notebook, 'a total of six second floor windows that would have had a viable angle of sight to shoot from. If only the victim had been shot. But no one is aware of anyone being in the right place at the right time. Apart from police officers. A few have mentioned one or more officers doing security checks that night.'

'That's right,' said Crawford. 'Immediately it happened, uniform did a sweep of the premises to check whether there was anyone on the upper floors who saw anything. We didn't get anything from that.'

'Okay,' said Vicky. 'It's technically possible one of the people in the premises could be lying and was on the upper floor at the time of the attack, but there's no evidence as yet. And Roland… I mean Doctor Mclean said Miss Levine wasn't killed with a gun, so I really can't see how someone could have taken a shot from one these windows.'

'That'll do for now,' said Crawford. 'Get back to the station and write it up.'

CHAPTER 5

FOUR WEEKS EARLIER

'That's very helpful,' said Capel. 'So, you think we've got a chance of making something of a literary festival here?'

'Indubitably,' said LeVine. 'I don't think the likes of Cheltenham or Hay have anything to worry about, but small, niche festivals – which is really all that we have in Marlborough – are drawing good crowds these days. It takes the right organiser, a well-chosen set of authors and a lot of work on publicity. But I'd have thought you would have a strong feed in from the Bath area – just make sure you stay well away from May, when the Bath Lit is on. There's nothing worse than a clash of festival dates. I'd consider September if it's next year, or November this year, to give enough time to get the word out.'

'Will people come out as late in the year as November?'

'It's actually quite a good time for the publishers – there's a shedload of books launched that time of year for the Christmas market. And there tends to be a social lull around then, before it all picks up for Christmas. It's an excellent opportunity to pull in the punters. Literary festivals may be about the arts, but you have to use a commercial brain.'

'That's great,' said Capel. He waved a sheet of paper at her. 'And thank you for the contact list – I wouldn't have known where to start.'

'It's the lovely thing about being in this business,' said LeVine. 'And as I suggested we always have to remember it is a business. The festivals aren't in competition with each other: the authors and the publishers love to have as many opportunities to show off as possible. Well, I say that the authors do – some display a distinct reluctance to promote themselves, but enough of them seem to enjoy a turn in the limelight to make it a rewarding, if taxing, enterprise for all. The most important thing, I'd suggest, is to get a good team together. Don't try to do it all on your own, it'll drag you down. I wouldn't have managed without a lot of help from my agent – and Suki, of course, my number two, though I think she'd rather she was the one who was calling the shots.'

'Thank you so much, said Capel. But I've taken up enough of your time on my idea.'

'Not at all. Oh, and one more thing I recommend, to avoid facing the wrath of the Society of Authors, not to mention Joanne Harris who is particularly vocal on the matter. Offer the authors a fee. It doesn't have to be huge, but all too often festival organisers expect the authors to perform for nothing. Without them there would be no festival, but somehow many festival organisers feel that it's acceptable to fob them off with talk of exposure and a bottle of wine. They'll quite happily pay the venue, or the caterers or whatever, but the poor old author is taken for granted as a free resource. The ideal is to give them a percentage of the take on the door. It's what they do for comedians, after all. Failing that, I'd say for the kind of small event you have in mind aim for around £150 a head.'

'Thanks again,' said Capel, scribbling notes. 'This is exactly the kind of detail I need.'

'Excellent. I'd love it if you could come over to Marlborough in a few weeks' time for the Mop, and we can go into more detail then. You're bound to have more questions once you've had a time to think it through.'

'The Mop?'

'Sorry, it's an ancient tradition we have in the town called a mop fair – there are two each year, a week apart. It used to be a venue for hiring workers – the housemaids, apparently, would carry a mop to show that was the job that they were looking for. These fairs have been run in Marlborough since the eighteenth century, if not earlier – but they gradually transformed into more of an entertainment, so now it's the usual travelling fairground rides and stalls, set up down the middle of the high street. They actually divert the A4 for it. Huge fun.'

'That would be excellent – perhaps I could bring my fiancée?'

'Of course, you must. The more the merrier, and I'd love to meet her. It is a her? One can't assume these days, but you being…'

'Yes, it's a her. And thanks, that's brilliant.' Capel hesitated, peering into his coffee cup. 'Erm, forgive me if it's intrusive, but is LeVine your real name or a nom de plume?'

LeVine laughed, her chins wobbling. 'Absolutely real. Though I must admit, I did start out in my first two books with a particularly dubious pen name. I was called Sally de Bayne.'

Capel snorted, suppressing a laugh. 'You are joking? As in the French?'

'No, it's really true – and congratulations. Not many people spot where the name came from without a little prompting. I overheard a couple from Margate use the phrase when asking for the toilet while on holiday in Le Touquet and I couldn't resist using it. But, for some reason I can no longer remember, I published what turned out to be my first really successful title under my own name, and after that, Sally was sent into well-deserved retirement.'

'Wonderful. But I mustn't keep distracting you. You were supposed to be here to research your new book.'

'Yes, of course – back to the day job. So, my new historical novel will span from the incident I read out to you from the Anglo-Saxon Chronicle to the next entry in the Chronicle where Bath was mentioned. Do you mind?' She held up her brown book again and leafed through to a yellow sticky note, used as a marker.

'Not at all,' said Capel.

'This is from the year 1013. "Then king Swein" – he was the Danish king at the time. Cnut, Canute as you probably know him, er, Swein was Cnut's dad – "Swein turned from, oh, er, that would be London, from London to Wallingford and so west across the Thames to Bath, where he stayed with his army. Swein had heard of the privy treasures of the Reeve Alfred, though this hoard could not be uncovered. Then Ealdorman Æthemaer" – he was from Devon, well, possibly – "came there, and with him the western thegns, and all submitted to Swein, and they gave him hostages. When he had fared thus, he then turned northward to his ships, and all the nation regarded him as full king."'

'Thanes?'

'Mm. With a G N at the end. As in Shakespeare – Thegn of Cawdor and all that. They were aristocratic underlings to royalty – a bit like ladies in waiting or gentlemen of the court. Posh types, part companion, part gofer and general dogsbody for the royals.'

'Okay,' said Capel. 'And what's the relevance of this chronicle entry?'

'As I said, it's Alfred's death and the circumstances surrounding it that are the key to my story. This is set back in 906, if you remember. But the Swein story gives us a fascinating hint that Alfred may have left something hidden, these "privy treasures" don't you see. What were they? And how would their rumoured existence have affected his family and local politics? This is the sort of detail that spawns the meat of historical fiction – that's a mixed metaphor, isn't it? You don't spawn meat. Sorry. It's the kind of thing where we know the basics, but there's a chance to fill in all the juicy details that make it possible to be both historically accurate and a page turner.'

'And Thornton Down comes into this how?'

'All the evidence is that Alfred's manor was in the vicinity of the village of Down. Here. His house would have been a good distance from Bath, as it was likely to have been based on a farm that had become rather grander over time. I was wondering if you had any church records in the village that go back to Anglo-Saxon times? Or just knowledge of any local legends that could tie into the story.'

'We can certainly take a look in the church,' said Capel, but it's going to be a long shot. All we've got here is an entirely nineteenth century building, not even one of the Victorians' so-called improvements of a medieval church – there was an earlier church building on the site, but the pre-Victorian records are extremely sparse. Have you got an hour or so to spare?'

'I'm at your disposal,' said LeVine.

'I'll just give someone a call who may be able to help us out on the local legend side. I haven't been here long enough to know all the ins and outs of village folklore.'

~

Peter Finch was already waiting by the church porch as Capel led LeVine up the path. The ageing parish treasurer had his head tilted back to catch the thin October sunlight on his lined face, his eyes closed against the brightness.

'Peter,' Capel said, 'thanks for getting here so quickly.'

Finch slowly lowered his face, adjusting his flat cap, his eyes still closed until the last moment. 'Aye, well, I was already in the churchyard when you rang. Tidying up a few graves.'

'Peter is more than just a treasurer,' Capel said to LeVine. 'He keeps this place running.'

'General purpose drudge,' said Finch, 'that's what I am.'

'We need people like you,' said LeVine. 'The country wouldn't be the same without your sound stock.'

Finch looked quickly from LeVine to Capel, as if to ask whether or not he should respond to the patronising tone. Capel shook his head. Finch wasn't noted for his diplomacy. 'After you, vicar,' said Finch, turning towards the doorway. Despite not seeing Finch's face, Capel knew there would be a broad smile on it. Finch had decided to take pity on Miss LeVine.

Capel led them through the building down to the vestry and opened the large old safe that sat rusting gently in the corner. 'As I said, we're quite limited in the historical documentation we have here. You may be able to find more at the county records office.' He pulled out a pile of thick books. Some of the covers were mouldy. 'There's the registers obviously. Oh, and this might be of interest.' He pulled a smaller, leather-bound notebook out from the corner of the safe behind a cash box. 'It has been with the parish for a couple of hundred years. A number of contributors have made notes on local history to a degree, but I think there's more the myths and legends of the place. To be honest, I've meant to read it properly for ages and never got round to it.'

'Oh, that's definitely of interest,' said LeVine, reaching for the book. 'This kind of material is priceless background material. You see, these country legends often have roots that go back for centuries.'

'You are welcome to take it with you as long as we get it back,' said Capel. 'For obvious reasons, I can't lend you the registers, but you can take a look through those here, and I can make a copy if you want anything.'

'Hmm?' said LeVine, flicking through the notebook. 'Oh, yes, this is excellent.'

'The registers?'

LeVine looked up for a moment. 'No, no, I don't think we need that at the moment. But this is something I can work with.' She turned back to the notebook, and read on until Finch gave an unsubtle cough. 'Sorry,' said LeVine. She gave them both a wide smile and pushed the notebook into her handbag. 'This kind of source is like catnip to a historical fiction author. Now, I gather that you are a unique source of local information, Mr Finch.'

'Shall we go back to the vicarage?' asked Capel. 'We don't have the heating on in the church at the moment, as you can tell.'

'Splendid,' said LeVine.

Back in his kitchen, Capel put the kettle on. It struck him that his job would be much harder without hot drinks to provide punctuation and lubrication. Finch and LeVine made themselves comfortable at the table.

'So, Mr Finch,' LeVine said, 'what can you tell me about local antiquities and legends?'

Finch scratched his head and reflexively reached for his pipe before remembering that smoking wasn't welcome in the vicarage. 'Well, the village has always had plenty of such stories. I remember when I were a lad being fond of Dildrum, King of the Cats. Then there's the Pace Egg play, the Combe Down treasure of course, and the story of Alfred's ruin.'

'Alfred?' said LeVine, at the same time as Capel said 'What? A Pace Egg play here?' Finch looked from one to the other. 'Why don't you just tell us about them your own way, Peter?' Capel asked. 'They all sound fascinating.'

Finch nodded. 'Well, Dildrum's a bloody stupid story – pardon my French, missus – but like I said, it appealed to me when I were a kid. Apparently, there was a gentleman in the olden days – quite possibly the vicar, as they were more likely to be gentlemen back then…' he paused for a carefully timed beat. 'No offence, Capel.'

'None taken.'

'Right. So, the vicar was sitting by the fire, reading a book when a cat rattled down the chimney, giving him quite a start. And this cat called out to him: "Tell Dildrum that Doldrum's dead!" then it headed out of the room, calm as you like. As you might imagine, the gentleman was quite taken aback. Just then, his wife came in, followed by their house cat, which they had called Mr Tiddles. The gentleman told his wife what had happened, and their cat's ears pricked up at his words. "Is Doldrum dead?" it asked. Then it shot up the chimney and was never seen again. Of course, no one knows for sure, but many think that the vicarage cat, Mr Tiddles, was really Dildrum, who had just discovered that the king of the cats had died, and he was now free to take up his royal inheritance. Like I said, silly stuff.'

'It's charming,' said LeVine. 'Probably too modern in origin to have a place in my book, but these legends can go back surprisingly far, particularly when they involve topics such as talking animals.'

'For years I kept an eye on our old moggie, in case it had royal tendencies or would talk, but it never showed any signs. And I remember, the first time we visited the vicarage here, I couldn't resist sticking my head up the chimney. It was a big open fire back then. Got covered in soot. My dad gave me good clattering.'

'You couldn't look up the chimney now,' Capel said to LeVine. 'It was blocked off in the sixties. Just a gas fire now. The tiles are supposed to be original, though.'

'Hmm,' said Finch. 'I heard later on that there were half a dozen villages around these parts that all claimed that the Dildrum, King of Cats thing had happened in their vicarage. It might make it seem unlikely it ever happened in Thornton, but you do wonder why that story was so widely spread.'

'Excellent,' said Capel. 'How about the Pace Egg play? I still remember some travelling players coming and putting one on in my junior school in Littleborough. But I thought it was a purely Lancashire tradition.'

'Pace Egg?' asked LeVine. 'I'm not familiar with the name, though presumably this was originally some kind of paschal egg, a performance for Easter?'

'Yes, it's a variant of a mummers' play,' said Capel. 'As you say, the name suggests that it was intended to be performed at Easter, but as I remember it, there was some mention of Christmas in the play itself, so it probably served a dual purpose.'

'That's it,' said Finch. 'It's a folk play, but I haven't seen one put on round here for thirty years or more. It has George and the Dragon, and a villain called Slasher.'

'Oh, yes,' said Capel. ' "I am a valiant soldier, and Slasher is my name. With sword and buckler by my side, I hope to win the game." I can't believe I can remember this from so long ago. I can still see it all in my mind's eye. Must be one of my strongest memories I have from junior school. When St George threatens to break Slasher's head, Slasher boasts "How canst thou break my head? Since it is made of iron, and my body's made of steel. My hands and feet are knuckle-bone: I challenge thee to feel!" Oh yes, and then when he gets hurt in the fight, there's a comedy doctor who claims to cure all sorts of things.'

Finch nodded. 'The itch, the pitch, the palsy and the gout: if a man gets nineteen devils in his skull, I'll cast twenty of them out. I have in my pockets crutches for lame ducks, spectacles for blind bumblebees, packsacks and panniers for grasshoppers and plaisters for broken-baked mice. Hey, Jack, have a sup from my bottle, and let it run down thy throttle. If thou be not quite slain, rise, Jack and fight again.'

'That's the one,' said Capel. I also seem to remember the whole thing gets more than a little politically incorrect with Prince Paradine and the King of Egypt involved before Beelzebub comes on, sends them all packing and threatens the audience with eternal damnation if they don't contribute generously to the players' beer money.'

LeVine applauded. 'Well done, both of you – I lived it, I really did. And to be fair, we do know that mummers and their plays go back at least as far as the thirteenth century, as they were noted as part of the Christmas wedding festivities of Edward the First's daughter. They could well have existed as far back as Anglo-Saxon times, but we don't know for sure. Even so, I could use one to add some colour. But what I'm particularly interested in, Mr Finch, are the last two items you mentioned. What was the Thornton Down treasure and what was the story of Alfred's ruin?'

'Combe Down treasure, not Thornton Down,' said Finch. 'And they're both part of one and the same legend. Combe Down's a bigger village, up the hill from here. They say that a thousand years or so ago a local bigwig by the name of Alfred was killed in a dispute with his neighbours. They didn't call in the police when the neighbours played music too loud back then. Alfred's family were left destitute, because their house was destroyed, and Alfred had thought that he'd been canny by hiding all his treasures… only once he were dead, no one else knew where he had hidden the gold, so his family starved.'

'Yes,' said LeVine to Capel, 'this sounds very promising indeed. It could well be the privy treasures that were mentioned in the Chronicle.'

'Really?' said Finch. 'I subscribe to the Chronicle, and I haven't seen anything about it. And I'm not sure how privies come into it.'

'Not the Bath Chronicle, Peter,' said Capel, 'the Anglo-Saxon Chronicle. Old records from a thousand years or so ago.'

'Ah.'

'Is anything said in the legend about the location of the hoard?' LeVine asked.

'Hmm,' said Finch. 'Yes and no. This Alfred was supposed to have had an estate south of Combe Down and west of here. Some kind of manor house, a big and fancy place for the time. The old stories don't say anything about where Alfred hid his treasure, because the whole point was that no one knew where it had been buried – that's why his family was ruined by his death. Apparently, when the kiddies died they were supposed to haunt the place. But…'

'What a shame, there's not more detail,' said LeVine. 'This was beginning to sound so promising. Though I suppose it does at least give us a vague location for the Reeve's holding. Would it be possible to visit the area, Mr Capel?'

'What, now?' said Capel. 'I'm afraid not. I'm due in Bath in an hour or so. But we could certainly arrange it another time. Having said that, there's a whole lot of open land and woodland between here and Combe Down. I mean, there are a couple of buildings, but if we're looking for the site of an Anglo-Saxon manor that was destroyed over a millennium ago, I think it would be a needle in a haystack thing. Obviously worth a hunt online, but I wouldn't hold my breath.'

'As it happens,' said Finch, 'I hadn't finished my story. Now, there used to be a railway line up that way, part of the old Somerset and Dorset railway. It started in Bath and ran round down through Midford, then Midsomer Norton and Burnham-on-Sea. From there you could go on all the way to Poole and Bournemouth. It were a lovely line, I went on it a few times as a kiddy with my gran, when they still had steam trains and compartments. After that, it was one of the lines that was axed by that bastard – excuse my French – that bastard Doctor Beeching in the sixties. The part of the old line that runs up through where we're talking about was turned into a cycle way and footpath. Quite popular it is, in the summer.'

'I know it,' said Capel. 'It is a nice path. Vicky and I've walked along there a few times, though I think the tunnels feels a bit creepy.'

'Tunnels?' said LeVine.

'Yes, there are two. The Combe Down tunnel's the most impressive. It's about a mile long. There are lights inside now and they play music in there… but it's still pretty dank and gloomy. Fun, though.'

'No ghosts?' said LeVine.

'Ah,' said Finch. 'There may be. You see, the tunnel has no ventilation shafts – it was the longest they ever built without 'em. There was an accident there in the 1920s. My dad told me about it. It was a particularly still, humid day, and the train, a freight train, was going very slowly and the crew passed out from the fumes. The train just chuntered on until it ran into the goods yard on the approach to Bath. Killed the driver and some workers there. But I suppose the ghosts would be in the tunnel if they were anywhere. Good company for Alfred's children.'

'That's fascinating, but is there any connection with the Alfred story?' asked Capel.

'I knew I'd mentioned the tunnel for some reason,' said Finch. 'They say that when it was being dug, the navvies found an old brooch. Inland navigators, they were, you know. Originally workers on the canals and then moved on to work on the railways. Anyway, this wasn't just old like a bit of junk, it were very old. The brooch ended up in Beckford's Tower, if you know where I mean. The navvies wanted to explore more, to see if there were more treasure to be found, but the bosses needed the tunnel to get finished quick like, and they never got a chance to find anything more.'

'I'd love to see that very old brooch,' said LeVine. 'Could we add this Beckford's Tower to my next visit?'

'Of course,' said Capel. 'I'm told it's a fascinating place, though I must admit I've never been. It's a folly alongside Lansdown Cemetery to the northwest of the city. Build by a George Beckford…'

'William Beckford, actually,' said Finch.

'Sorry, yes, you probably know this better than me, Peter.'

'I doubt it, I haven't been there either. But we were told about William Beckford when I was at school. Very rich man, he was, supposed to be the richest man in the whole country who wasn't a proper member of the aristocracy. Owned quite a bit of

Lansdown Crescent, and he had a long ride constructed, all the way up to Lansdown where he built this tower, in 1820 something. Beckford were a bit of a collector, which I imagine is how the brooch ended up there. One of your arty, dodgy characters, if you take my drift.'

'Does that work chronologically?' asked Capel. 'I didn't think the Liverpool and Manchester opened until the 1830s, and this tunnel must have been built considerably later.'

'That's right,' said Finch. 'The tunnel was dug in 1870 or so. Well after Beckford died. But I believe they were still adding stuff to the bits of his collection that weren't sold off for some time after his death.'

'Fascinating,' said LeVine. 'And to think all most people know about Bath is the Romans, Beau Brummel and Jane Austen.'

~

PRESENT DAY

Capel watched as Vicky spread clotted cream on a scone, then topped it with jam. He shook his head. 'I'm sure last time we had scones you did it the correct way. Jam first, then cream.'

'How I choose to eat my scones, said Vicky, 'is my affair.' She stressed the word 'scones' rhyming it with 'cones', where Capel had rhymed it with 'cons'. Vicky licked a spot of cream from her fingertip. 'Anyway, what do you know? You're a northerner, but I wasn't far from Devon when I lived in Glastonbury.'

'I holidayed in Cornwall a lot as a boy,' said Capel, 'and they know which way up to spread their scones there.'

Vicky shook her head. 'So, how did it go with the E-FIT? I think it was a good idea to stay in Marlborough for this. I'd have been starving if we'd had to drive home first. I didn't get any lunch.'

'It wasn't too bad, though the mugshots they produce always look like a series of cartoon villains to me. Or something off that Guess Who game where you have to match pairs of faces. More caricature than likeness. What I produced could bear a passing resemblance to the fake Russell Levine. Or equally possibly to some dodgy character off Eastenders.' He waved to a passing waitress, who topped up his coffee. 'I can't decide which I like best here, the breakfast or the afternoon tea. Which do you think is better?'

Vicky looked around the crowded interior of the Polly Tea Room as if she expected to see something or someone she recognised. 'Okay, which of your harem did you bring here last time? Because it certainly wasn't me who had breakfast with you. I've never been here before in my life.'

'Ah,' said Capel. He pensively took a bite of scone, wiping the oozing jam from the corner of his mouth. 'No. I mean, yes. Come to think of it, I was on my own. It was only a few days after we first met, and I was driving up from Glastonbury to Uffington at the time. I stopped off here for lunch, but I couldn't resist their all-day breakfast. You know me and a cooked breakfast. I mean, they have fried potatoes.'

Vicky poked Capel's stomach. 'I know you only too well. I'll let you off. It is a nice place. Just about on the acceptable side of twee.' She pushed her chair back a little so that she could see past the other tables to the front window. Outside, shoppers bustled past in the fading afternoon light. 'And it's a good place for people watching.'

'Absolutely,' said Capel. He pointed to an elderly lady, plodding slowly passing, pulling a tartan shopping basket on wheels behind her. 'That one, for instance. You wouldn't think butter would melt in her mouth, but she's like one of the characters from *Arsenic and Old Lace* who take in lonely men as lodgers and cheerfully poison them to put them out of their misery. She is very kind to cats, though.'

'Mm, mm,' said Vicky, washing down her scone with some tea. 'And that couple with the dog, they're renowned jewel thieves, scouting the location for their next heist. They think Marlborough is the idea place to remain anonymous, because it's always full of strangers.'

'That's a good one,' said Capel. 'Now this guy coming over from the left he's… someone who impersonates a dead woman's nephew.'

'Sorry?'

'It's him,' Capel said, pushing back his chair so quickly it teetered and nearly fell into the lap of the American couple behind him. 'Sorry.' He grabbed Vicky's arm. 'It's the fake Russell.'

'Shit!' said Vicky. She scrabbled her warrant card out of her bag as they hurried towards the door. 'Sorry, police,' she said quickly to the waitress. 'We have to catch up with someone, but we'll be back to pay.'

A large family of six was working its way slowly into the café through the doorway leading to the narrow shop section that made up the entrance. 'Excuse me!' said Vicky. 'Police! Coming through.' She waved the warrant card at them and squeezed through the narrow gap between the mother and the largest of the sons. Capel smiled apologetically and wormed his way through after her.

The delay had cost precious seconds. When Capel got out onto the pavement Vicky was standing by the roadside, glaring at him. 'Which one?' she said.

Capel peered along the street to the right of the entrance. 'There,' he said. 'Thinnish bloke with short brown hair. Turning right through that passageway.'

'Got him,' said Vicky. She sprinted down the street, dodging the slow walkers, with Capel close behind. Capel's 'passageway' proved to be an opening wide enough for a single car, an alleyway that passed through the building, coaching inn style, and led down to the town's main car park. Just as Vicky reached it, a big Audi SUV pulled off the High Street into the opening. The car was so wide there was no room to get past on the narrow footway.

'Careful!' said Capel.

'Shift, you idiot!' Vicky shouted at the driver. The moment there was clearance at the side of the car she pounded through the opening and down to the car park. There was no sign of the man. Capel panted to a stop beside her. 'Can you see him?' Vicky asked.

Capel shook his head, struggling to speak.

'I'll try in Waitrose,' Vicky said, pointing to the back of the supermarket, 'and you go down and check the rest of the car park.'

'And what do I do if I find him?'

'Stay on him, but don't approach him. Give me a call and let me handle it.'

'Roger, boss.'

Vicky pushed past a couple of people who were negotiating trolleys out of the smart red brick rear of the supermarket and scanned the inside of the store. There was no one who looked anything like her brief glimpse of the fake Russell Levine. She quickly zigzagged up and down the aisles. It was useless. He wasn't inside the shop.

Jogging out, she found Capel, heading back from the overflow section of the car park, reached across a small bridge over the River Og. He shook his head before he was in earshot. 'No, sorry,' he said as Vicky closed in on him. 'He's gone.'

Vicky growled. 'Shit,' she said again.

'I'm really sorry.'

'It's not your fault. At least we know that he's linked to Miss LeVine through Marlborough. That'll be useful for the local plod to know when they put out your E-FIT. That kind of thing always works better if you can pin down the search area. I'll head over to the station and fill them in.'

'Okay,' said Capel. 'I'd better nip back to the Polly Tea Room and pay. I don't suppose we can claim this on expenses now that it's turned out to be part of an investigation?'

Vicky raised an eyebrow.

'Fair enough. It was worth a try. I'll meet you at the cop shop.'

CHAPTER 6

The front door slammed as Vicky headed back in after her morning run. 'You really should come with me, you could do with the exercise,' she shouted to Capel, who was peering suspiciously into their newly acquired bread maker.

'I don't think so,' said Capel. 'First of all, you'd show me up and either race on ahead of me or moan about having to run slowly for my benefit, and secondly I prefer a fast walk. It's just as good as exercise if it's quick enough and it is far less damaging to the joints.'

'Whatever,' said Vicky. 'I'm having a quick shower, then I've got to head back over to Marlborough. They've asked me to interview Margaret's deputy on the Literary Festival. Want to come with?'

'Why not,' said Capel. 'I like Marlborough. Have you seen the instructions for this bread maker thing? I thought I'd try making a loaf.'

'They're in the usual drawer. But we haven't got any bread flour.'

'I'm sure that's the sort of thing they'll have in Marlborough. They're bound to stock all possible knit-your-own-yoghurt stuff there. It's not a hippy place like Glastonbury, but it's distinctly upmarket Friends of the Earth.'

Vicky snorted and jogged up the stairs.

~

After driving twice around the block, they found a place to park at the end of the narrow Silverless Street at the north end of the town and walked around the corner and down the hill to a quaint cottage on Marlborough's small green. Capel stood back as Vicky checked her notebook to make sure it was the right house and rapped on the door.

A woman in her late thirties or early forties answered. 'Yes?'

Vicky recognised the 'Not Jehovah's Witnesses again?' look and spoke quickly. 'Hello, my name is Detective Constable Denning…' she held up her warrant card, 'and this is the Reverend Capel who is helping us with our enquiry into Margaret LeVine's death. Are you Mrs Sukie Dawson?'

'Ms,' the woman said. 'Yes, please come in. It's terrible. Things like that don't happen in Marlborough.'

They followed her into a low-ceilinged sitting room, so modern and minimalist that it seemed as if they had passed through a portal into a totally different building from the classic cottage exterior. 'Can I get you anything to drink?' said Dawson. 'Tea, coffee? A glass of something?'

'Coffee would be lovely, thank you,' said Vicky. 'Can I help?'

'No, no, that's fine. It was on already – it will only take a moment. Please do sit down.'

Vicky perched on the edge of an armchair, while Capel sat back on the sofa. 'Do you want me to ask her anything?' Capel said quietly.

Vicky shook her head. 'I mean, I'm not saying stay entirely silent, I know you're not capable of that. But leave the important questions to me. Stick to making sympathetic noises.' She flicked to a blank page in her notebook.

'Here we are,' said Dawson, re-emerging with a tray loaded with the paraphernalia of coffee, including a cafetière and a plate of Bahlsen chocolate biscuits.

'Mm, my favourite,' said Capel.

'Do you usually bring a vicar with you?' Dawson asked Vicky.

'Not as a matter of routine,' said Vicky. 'But Capel was present when Miss LeVine died and has been helping us by providing support for those who have been impacted by her death. I gather you worked with her on the Literary Festival, Ms Dawson.'

'Call me Suki, please. Yes. Margaret liked to keep a firm hand on the tiller, ever since she took on the festival, years before we moved to Marlborough. My husband works in London: he tends to stay in our flat up in town during the week, but I wanted to live somewhere more pleasant and relaxing. We've been hoping to start a family for a while. Sorry, I'm rambling. That's got nothing to do with Margaret. Yes, so when we moved here, I was looking for a way to contribute to the community, and the literary festival seemed an ideal opportunity to make use of my talents. I used to work in publishing, you see.'

'Of course,' said Vicky. 'How did you find Miss LeVine was to work with?'

'I'll be honest, she was not the easiest co-worker. She liked to be in control of everything, every little detail. And whenever we got anyone remotely famous in as a speaker, she was all over them like a rash. I hardly got a look in, although I did all the legwork for some of the best catches we had. It was I who got Joanne Harris, for example. You know, *Chocolat*? But ever since, Margaret talked as if Joanne was her best friend. Sorry, that sounds awful, speaking about the dead like that, but I think it's important that I am totally honest with the police.'

'So do I,' said Vicky. 'It's very important.'

'Will you be taking over the festival?' asked Capel, earning himself a sharp look from Vicky.

'Well, yes, I suppose I will,' said Dawson. 'I did wonder if we ought to cancel next year's event out of respect, but we've already started booking the authors, and in the end, it's a far better way of remembering Margaret to put it on, rather than to cancel it, don't you think? I feel it's what she would have wanted. We will make sure that it is very much a memorial to her and her sterling work over the years.'

'Is there anyone else who might take charge?' asked Vicky.

'Oh, no. No, definitely not. It was very much the two of us at the top – a double act, you might say – and now the burden has fallen on me. I've got plenty of helpers, of course, but it's entirely up to me to uphold Margaret's wonderful legacy.'

Vicky nodded. 'Can you think of anyone who might want to harm Miss LeVine?'

Dawson paused to take a sip of her coffee, her eyes on the ceiling. 'Gosh, that's such a hard question to answer. Margaret could certainly rub people up the wrong way, there's no doubt about that. She was lovely as long as you went along with her ideas, but any attempt to say anything different, to come up with something new, and she could get very prickly. I think that's why she wasn't elected Police and Crime Commissioner.'

'She stood for election?' said Vicky.

Dawson nodded. 'Oh yes, earlier this year. It wasn't her politics that put people off. She was very strong on dealing with police corruption and incompetence, which everyone should be concerned about. But the way she put it across simply rubbed people up the wrong way. If you want to get into politics you need to be more… approachable, rather than domineering, I think.'

'Was there anyone in particular she rubbed up the wrong way?' asked Vicky.

'I know she had a bit of a run-in with that Smith man, the one who's our local history bore. He had a tendency to correct her online, nit-picking at little details in her books, which she obviously found infuriating.'

'Smith man?' said Capel.

'Mm. Can't remember his first name at the moment, but you'll find him all over the place online. Considers himself the foremost expert on Marlborough history, and he takes an interest in the Bath area as well, which wound Margaret up, as she was intending to feature it in her next book. Oh, yes, and speaking of books, you need to get in touch with Cherie Taylor. She's a historical fiction type like Margaret was – something of a competitor. And Cherie was decidedly peeved with Margaret earlier this year. Cherie had a new book out and wanted to appear at the festival to promote it. Margaret turned her down flat. She said we'd already filled the schedule, but I know that just wasn't true. She, Margaret I mean, she didn't want to give any publicity to her rival.'

'Authors,' said Capel. 'A dangerous breed.'

'So true,' said Dawson. 'It'd be much easier if you

could run a literary festival without the authors, but unfortunately, they're a necessary evil.' Her smile, intended to show she was joking, was not entirely convincing.

'And Ms Taylor would know that Miss LeVine was responsible for excluding her from the festival?' asked Vicky.

'Sadly, someone seems to have leaked the information to Cherie,' said Dawson. 'It was very unprofessional, but what can you do? We never got to the bottom of who was responsible.'

Vicky nodded. Capel could see that she was trying to suppress a smile. 'Is there anyone else we should talk to?'

'No one specifically connected to the festival,' said Dawson. 'There were bound to be other people she wound up, because, as I say, she could be difficult, but most of them took it in their stride, like that lovely nephew of hers, Russell. You don't come across many Russells these days, do you? The name seems to have gone out of fashion.'

'You know Russell Levine?' asked Capel.

'I've met him a few times at festival events and I see him around. Marlborough's not a big place. He's – he was very devoted to his aunt.'

'That's all very helpful,' said Vicky. 'Thank you. I'm sorry to have to ask, but it's routine – I'm sure you understand. Where were you the night that Miss LeVine died? Last Saturday, the seventeenth. The night of the Small Mop. Say between five and nine.'

'Of course, you have to ask,' said Dawson. 'I find the whole Mop thing rather wearing. It brings in entirely the wrong kind of people. A lot of them come from Swindon, which says it all. I stayed at home all evening with a bottle of red and a DVD. Much more pleasant than venturing down to the High Street.'

'Can anyone back that up?' asked Vicky. 'Your husband, perhaps?'

'No, I'm sorry, Paul was away on business for the weekend. In Scotland, you see.'

'Did you cook that night?' asked Capel.

'You know, I didn't,' said Dawson. 'So of course, someone did see me in the evening – the lovely man who delivers for the Raj, round in Kingsbury Street. He'll be able to confirm that I placed the order.'

'Thank you,' said Vicky. 'We won't take up any more of your time, but we may have to call back at some point.'

Once they were outside, Capel nudged her. 'How about a walk round to the Raj? They're probably opening for lunch around now and it's ages since we had an Indian.'

'Really? I suppose we could at least call in and ask about their delivery driver. What did you think of "call me Suki" Dawson?'

'Clearly happy to have Margaret LeVine out of the way to get her hands on the festival. That doesn't make her a killer, but I certainly wouldn't rule her out. These literary types can be vicious. It's certainly worth following up on the local historian and the rival author.'

'Yes, we've already got Cherie Taylor in our sights, but this Mr Smith is worth looking up.' Vicky peered at her phone. 'What road did she say the Indian was in?'

'Kingsbury Street.'

'Got it – just round the corner in that windy back

street.'

'Okay, I… hang on.' Capel pulled his own phone out. 'It's Russell Levine. The real one, I mean. The fake didn't leave his number. Hello?'

Vicky watched Capel's expression change slightly as he went into what she thought of as his professional mode.

'It's not a problem. To be honest, I'd forgotten,' Capel said into the phone. He listened again. 'Okay, how about Friday morning? If you can come over to the vicarage about 10? – Excellent, I'll see you then.' He put the phone away. 'I'd totally forgotten, Levine had asked about visiting a couple of the locations his aunt had mentioned. He was supposed to be coming over today. It's a good job he turned out to be busy or he'd be waiting for me back in Thornton Down.'

'Can I join you when comes over Friday?'

'Of course – that makes a lot of sense. Where did you say the restaurant was?'

'Just round the corner there.'

The Raj had already opened, but there were no diners inside. A waiter emerged from a door at the back as they entered. 'Hello? Table for two?'

'No, we…' Vicky saw Capel's face. 'Yes, okay, a quick lunch would be good, but I can't take much time.'

'I can eat quickly,' said Capel.

'Would it be possible to have a word with the manager?' Vicky asked as the waiter presented them with menus.

The waiter looked concerned. 'Is there a problem?'

'No, not at all,' said Vicky. 'It's nothing to do with our visit today, it's about something else.'

The waiter shrugged. He went through to the

back. A few moments later an older man with a white beard came out. 'Yes? Can I help you?'

Vicky produced her warrant card. 'I am Detective Constable Denning. We are making some enquiries linked to a recent death.' Vicky saw the fear on the man's face and hurriedly went on: 'The death was not connected in any way to food supplied from your restaurant. I just need to find out about a delivery that you may have made on Saturday.'

'Of course, let me get the book.'

'He looked terrified,' said Capel.

'I suppose it wasn't the most tactful thing to say. It just never occurred to me he'd think we were accusing them of poisoning someone.'

Capel grinned. 'Should be worth at least a free beer.'

The manager returned with a large, battered old book. 'Here we are, Saturday the seventeenth. What are we looking for?'

'An order for a house on the Green. Name of Dawson.'

'Hmm, yes, one of our regulars for deliveries.' The manager flicked back a page and ran his finger down the orders. 'Here we are, yes, there was an order for 8pm. Onion bhajis, chicken tikka balti, lamb dopiaza, Bombay aloo and pilau rice. We threw in poppadums. We always throw in poppadums.'

'It's a big order for one person,' Capel muttered.

Vicky jotted in her notebook. 'Do you know who made the delivery?'

'I'm sure I can find that.' The manager squinted at the page. 'Sorry, the handwriting is absolutely terrible. And I really do need to get a new pair of spectacles. Erm, yes, it was Rashid.'

'He wouldn't happen to be in today?'

'He is – he washes up when he's not doing the deliveries.'

'Could we have a quick word with him?'

'He's not in trouble, is he? He's my cousin's son. He's not a bad young man.'

'No, really, we're just checking on the details of this delivery. It has nothing to do with Rashid.'

'I'll fetch him.'

Capel watched the manager disappear round the corner. 'Naan or rice?'

'Definitely naan.'

'Correct answer.'

The manager came back with a man in his early twenties, dressed in jeans and a T-shirt. 'This is Rashid.'

'There's nothing to worry about,' said Vicky. 'I just wonder if you remember making a delivery on the Green at 8pm last Saturday? For a Ms Dawson.'

Rashid looked at the entry in the order book. 'Yeah, I've been there a few times. She usually tips me. Not many of them do.'

'Did she tip you on Saturday?' asked Capel.

Rashid shook his head. 'I didn't see her. Some bloke answered the door.'

'Her husband?' asked Vicky. 'Would you know if it was her husband?'

Rashid shook his head again. 'Nah, I know him. He's a tight so… customer. He never tips. No, it wasn't him. A younger bloke. I didn't know him. Shorter than the husband, but I can't remember anything else about him. Ordinary looking.'

'Thanks so much,' said Vicky.

'Could I take your order?' said the manager, 'If

you're ready.'

'Why not,' said Capel. When they'd ordered and been brought beers and poppadums he took a generous dip in the mango chutney and raised his eyebrows at Vicky. 'So, our Suki was fibbing, then? Not a solitary meal with a glass of red after all. I was a bit suspicious when she said that. Red wine doesn't go well with a curry.'

'Hmm,' said Vicky. 'We've certainly a few questions for her to answer. We don't know that she was there after all – her alibi has just fallen apart if she didn't answer the door – and who was the mystery man who did?'

'Should we pop round after this?'

'She can stew for a bit.'

'Hmm. What do you think about this Police and Crime Commissioner business? Could this have been an inside job from your lot? You said your Marlborough colleagues were a mixed bunch, performance-wise. Maybe one of them fell nicely into that "incompetent" bracket call-me-Suki mentioned. Does this make a police officer a suspect? Or perhaps it was a conspiracy between everyone at the police station?'

Vicky pulled a face. 'It's not Line of Duty.' Before she could say more, her phone rang. She held up a hand to Capel. 'Denning?'

Capel smiled at the waiter who had brought out a collection of dishes. 'Lovely, thank you.' He helped himself and Vicky to generous portions.

'Okay,' Vicky said down the phone. 'Yes, I will.' She scribbled in her notebook. 'Where? North London? Okay, thanks. I'm sure he will. Bye.'

Capel looked at her but didn't speak.

'Stop looking so bloody patient,' said Vicky. 'It's sickening and it doesn't suit you.'

'Sorry,' said Capel.

'As it happens, you can do something to help.'

'Well, that's kind of me.'

'I've got a follow-up to track down this Smith.'

'Ah. The Smith man.'

'Precisely. It's a bit of a drive, so you could do me a big favour. We need to get some background from Miss LeVine's editor: you know, her contact at her publisher. The Inspector's suggested that I ask you to visit her. Just to get the basics. It's irregular, but they're really pushed for resources here even with me helping. And if a professional did it, we'd have to get the nod from the Met, but if you go, well, it's not our problem, is it? We can't be held responsible for the actions of a rogue vicar.'

'Sneaky,' said Capel. 'And this editor's based in North London?'

'How? Of course, the phone. Yes, she is. Do you mind? We just need to know about this Patel woman's relationship with Miss LeVine and where she was on Saturday evening.'

'Of course I don't mind. Would it be a problem if I look up Ed while I'm up there? I haven't seen him for ages.'

'What? No. Why would it be a problem? Take him with you to see Ms Patel. Maneet Patel, it is.' She paused to find a scrap of paper and jotted down an address and telephone number from her notebook. 'Safety in numbers: Ed'll protect you if she's fierce, and he's always been smooth with the ladies.'

'Really? Smooth with the ladies? You make him sound like Terry Thomas in one of those black and white 1950s comedies.'

Vicky smiled briefly. 'I said to tell her you'd ring to confirm a time, but she'll be in the office until late.'

'Thanks,' said Capel. 'There isn't a train station in Marlborough, is there?'

'No,' said Vicky. 'I'll drop you at Swindon station then get back down here. As soon as we've finished eating.'

CHAPTER 7

The train slid into Paddington station on time. Capel waited while the more hurried passengers had got off before fastening his coat and stepping onto the platform. Looking at the depressed-looking travellers ahead of him, Capel thought as he had many times before how lucky he was not to have to commute every day.

As soon as he got through the barrier, he saw the tall figure of Ed Ridge heading towards him. 'Dead on time,' Ed said as he hugged Capel. 'It must be divine intervention. Have we time for a coffee and a catchup?'

Capel smiled. 'Afterwards. I rang Ms Patel from the train. We're due there in half an hour. It's Islington – I'm not sure how long it'll take to get there.'

'Where in Islington?'

'North Road.'

'Hmm, Caledonian Road tube, then. Circle and Piccadilly. It'll take about 25 minutes. It's tight but doable. You can fill me in with a bit more detail on the way.'

'Great,' said Capel, used to his friend's unerring ability to navigate public transport anywhere in London off the top of his head. 'Lead the way, oh metropolitan sage.'

'I forget what a yokel you've become,' said Ed. 'You can be my apprentice. This way, young Capel. There is much for you to learn here in the great wen.'

~

The office building in North Road looked like a converted factory.

'Suitably trendy for a publisher – post-industrial chic,' said Ed.

'I was thinking their offices would be somewhere more big and scary,' said Capel. 'Like something out of *Metropolis*. The silent film, I mean, not where Clark Kent lives.'

'That'd only have been the case if it had been one of the big five,' said Ed. 'Or is it four? However many mega-publishers there are now. They keep buying each other. This one's not in that league.'

There was no one at the building's reception desk. Capel and Ed followed a sign to take the stairs for the second floor, where there was a separate reception for LeVine's publisher, Encaustic Books. 'I've an appointment with Ms Patel,' said Capel. 'The name's Capel.'

The receptionist stroked his shaved head and stared at Ed. 'What about him?'

'He's with me,' said Capel.

The receptionist shrugged. 'Nobody's perfect.' He picked up the phone, pressed a key and waited. 'Your four thirty.' He waited a moment, nodded slowly as if the person he was speaking to could see him and put the phone down. 'Take a seat please.' He pointed to an uncomfortable-looking leather sofa by a low coffee table where the day's newspapers were piled.

Ed strode over and collapsed onto the couch, peering at the newspapers on offer. He reached for the top one.

'Do you think you should?' asked Capel. 'Have you noticed how carefully they're all aligned. I bet he measures them to get the edges straight. After he's ironed them.'

Ed looked across at the receptionist and smiled, then picked up the Guardian from the top of the pile and knocked the others so they scattered across the table. 'Oops,' he said.

Capel shook his head. 'That was cruel and unnecessary.'

'Nobody's perfect,' said Ed. He scanned the headlines. 'I don't often get a chance to read the Guardian – the department only provides the Times and the FT – for the rest, we just get a summary from whatever you call the electronic version of a cutting service.'

'It's embarrassing,' said Capel, 'but the last time I regularly read a newspaper was when I was at school. It feels more like something my parents' generation would do – but I still feel guilty about it. Actually, I did get a subscription to the *i* newspaper once, but I didn't renew it. I enjoy reading a newspaper occasionally as a treat, but when I had one every day, it felt like a chore. Something I had to read because I'd paid for it.'

'Mr Capel?'

Capel jumped – he had been trying to read the headlines on the back of Ed's newspaper and hadn't heard anyone approaching.

'Sorry, I startled you.'

Capel stood and turned. For some reason, he'd expected a book editor to be relatively old, but Maneet Patel was almost certainly younger than he was. 'Not at all. It's just Capel, if that's okay. And this is my former colleague, Ed Ridge. I hope you don't mind, but I took the opportunity of being in London to look Ed up, and he insisted on tagging along.'

'No problem,' said Patel. She led them through an open-plan office to a glass-walled meeting room, mostly clear glass with a frosted panel in the middle etched with the names of Victorian authors. Along one wall was a waist-high bookcase with a dozen or so hardbacks, each positioned face forward. Two of them had Margaret LeVine's name on the cover.

'Would you mind if I recorded our conversation?' Capel asked, putting his phone on a coffee table in the centre of the room. 'It would be less obtrusive than taking notes.'

'That's fine,' said Patel. 'I'm not going to be giving out any trade secrets.'

They sat in armchairs by the table and accepted the offer of coffee. 'Why Encaustic?' asked Ed as Patel operated the Nespresso machine. 'It sounds like something to do with tiles.'

'The MD really wanted to make it Iconic Books, but that was too close to the name of an existing publishing house. She collects Russian Orthodox icons. But I think Encaustic works better. We specialise in genre fiction, and to me "Encaustic" sounds more genre.'

'Sorry,' said Capel, 'what's genre fiction? I don't have a publishing background.'

'Well, no, I suppose not,' said Patel with a nod to Capel's dog collar. 'Broadly, fiction tends to be divided into literary and genre. Literary is the worthy, snobby part with most of the posh prizes and media coverage, but relatively small sales apart from the odd exception, while genre is the enjoyable bit of the market that actually sells. We specialise in historical and crime fiction, though the genre segment also includes science fiction, fantasy and the like.'

'I gather there are still prizes in genre fields, though,' said Capel. 'I hear that Margaret was up for one of them for her latest. The Walter Scott prize, was it?'

'Of course, yes,' said Patel. 'We have our token prizes, at least one for each genre. And, to be fair, we ought to recognise that sometimes a genre title can break out to be recognised by the lit fic snobs. Hilary Mantel is the obvious example – two Bookers for what was definitely historical fiction. But we remain very much the poor cousin of the literary brigade. It's not true of Mantel, but all too often when a genre fiction novel becomes more widely popular, the author denies it was ever genre in the first place. Margaret Atwood's probably the worst example. There's no doubt that her *Handmaid's Tale* was science fiction, for example, but she denies it. I didn't hear it myself, but apparently in a BBC interview she claimed that science fiction was limited to "talking squids in outer space." It's a bizarre cliché, like suggesting that literary fiction is only concerned with the existential angst of privileged middle-class, middle-aged, white people. Sorry. It's a hobbyhorse of mine.'

'Don't apologise,' said Ed. 'I absolutely agree. Nine times out of ten "literary" just means dull or worthy. Or both at the same time.'

'The lovely science fiction writer Ursula K. Le Guin said something rather wonderful about Atwood's attitude.' Patel picked up her phone and scrolled through some text. 'She said that Attwood's viewpoint seems to be "designed to protect her novels from being relegated to a genre still shunned by hidebound readers, reviewers and prize-awarders. She" – Attwood, that is, in Le Guin's words – "doesn't want the literary bigots to shove her into the literary ghetto." So, gentlemen, welcome to the dark heart of the literary ghetto.' She shook her head. 'I really am sorry, though. You came to talk about Margaret, not to get a lecture on the kind of inferiority complex that comes from being a genre publisher.'

'It's still valuable background,' said Capel. 'As I mentioned to your colleague on the phone, I was with Margaret when she was killed. I'm helping the police informally – they just asked if I could get a little background on Margaret and those she would have dealt with as far as the publishing part of her life went.'

'There's a strong tradition of investigative clergymen,' said Patel, 'though we haven't got any on our list at the moment. Have you ever thought of writing a novel? Sorry, going off piste again. As you can see, Margaret was a valued author.' She pointed to the books behind her. '*The Rose and the Thorn* there is the title that's up for the Walter Scott, though I'm not sure what's going to happen with that now.'

'So you don't just put out a different selection of books each time you have a visitor to impress them?' asked Ed.

'That's very cynical, Mr, erm, sorry?'

'Ridge. No, it's me who should be sorry. Is it good for business?'

'Is what good for business?'

'Having a dead author. I know that when a musician dies there's often a surge in sales of their work.'

'I suppose, yes, the publicity that goes with unexpected death can help move copies. But Margaret was very popular anyway. And I thought of her as a friend.'

'She was popular,' said Capel quickly, trying to take the edge off the conversation. 'I loved her books. Would you say that she had any obvious rivals? Other historical fiction authors, perhaps, who might now benefit from her demise in terms of their own sales?'

'Oh, come on, Capel,' said Patel with a grin. 'This isn't Midsomer Murders, you know. Of course, there are other authors who have envied Margaret's success, but it's about as likely as a fellow vicar finishing you off because they were jealous of the success of your sermons.'

Capel nodded. 'True, that's always a danger in my profession. So, would you say that Margaret was popular with her peers?'

'Well,' said Patel, pausing to take a sip of her espresso, 'I wouldn't go that far. If you knew her, you'll know that she was a generous woman, but also a very driven individual. Having a conversation with her always felt like you were being interviewed for her research. And she was passionate about maintaining high standards in her craft, which meant that she wrote some reviews of the work of other historical fiction authors that were less than, erm, complimentary. Look up her Sunday Times review of Cherie Taylor's latest. To call Margaret's opinion barbed does not do it justice.'

Capel nodded. 'And was it a reasonable assessment?'

'Sorry?' said Patel.

'Was she fair in her opinion of Cherie Taylor's work?'

'Yes, I'd say so. But then I would, wouldn't I? Taylor isn't one of our authors.'

'How did you find Miss LeVine?' asked Ed.

'Through her agent,' said Patel. 'It's the usual way.' She snorted. 'Sorry, I couldn't resist that. I found her entirely professional. I might have been exaggerating a little to call her a friend, but she was a good business partner, which in the end is the only way the relationship between an author and a publisher can be framed. When your editor gets overly close you've become too famous and your output will suffer. Take a look at any successful author whose books suddenly balloon to twice the length of her original bestsellers. Margaret was picky, but she was also reliable. I've never known her deliver a manuscript late, which, frankly, is a rarity in this business.'

'In what sense was she picky?' asked Capel.

'Always concerned with detail. I think it's a necessary characteristic to be a really good historical fiction author. They check and re-check every little description in their book. Would someone have used those words back then? Had that piece of clothing been introduced yet? Was it acceptable for someone of the character's class to wear it? And that concern for detail extended into her business dealings. LeVine's agent can be rather amateurish when it comes to checking the detail. Frankly, he isn't very good at reading the fine print of contracts. He loves doing deals, but he can't be bothered with dotting the i's and crossing the t's. A bit of a chancer, if you know what I mean, though he makes an excellent dinner companion. LeVine's had to point out errors in contracts to him – when we accidentally omitted an escalator clause, for example.'

'Escalator clause?' said Ed. 'Is that the writer's equivalent of a musician's riders? You know, where they insist on having a bowl of yellow M and Ms in the dressing room or whatever. So, are we saying that there are authors who demand only to stay in hotels that have escalators?'

'Not exactly,' said Patel. 'It just means the author gets a bigger percentage of the profit on a book in their royalties if we sell over a certain number of copies. And Margaret actually read her royalty statements, line by line. She even used a spreadsheet to check them. We had an instance where we'd listed more returns than sales for a particular format, which she picked up on, much to our embarrassment.'

'Sorry?' said Capel.

'I'm the one who should be sorry, bombarding you with these technical details. It really doesn't matter.'

'No, please,' said Capel, 'I'm fascinated. There's something romantic about the publishing business.'

'If you insist, though romance doesn't enter into it. Books go out to bookstores on a sale or return basis. It's a business nightmare, but it's hard to see how we can get out of it now. In our statements we show the number of books "sold" but then we subtract from those numbers any books that are returned, in order to reach the real sales figure. Unfortunately, the returns can lag months or even years behind the original sales. And, of course, a book could well go out in hardback and then later in paperback, or it could start as a trade paperback then be issued in a mass market format. We'd made a cock-up and recorded some mass market returns as trade, which are worth more. Embarrassingly, this made it look as if more trade paperbacks had been returned than had been sent out in the first place. We had to grovel to Margaret after that one.'

'So, was she thinking of going elsewhere?' said Ed. 'To another publisher?'

'Good grief, no,' said Patel. 'We got on wonderfully. The relationship of an editor with her author can be a very close one. The business with the royalty statements was years ago, before I was here, when we still did the calculations ourselves on a spreadsheet. It's all automated now.'

'That's good,' said Capel. 'One thing the police did ask is if I could check with you where you were on Saturday. It's just a routine check – they're asking everyone who knew Margaret. If you're not happy with me asking they can…'

'Of course, no, that's fine,' said Patel. 'I was actually supposed to be going down to Marlborough myself that evening to see Margaret. She'd invited me to the fair, but I couldn't go in the end. Bit of a cat crisis. I spent most of the evening at the vet.'

'Nothing serious, I hope?' said Ed.

'Not as it turned out, but my cat was hit by a car. She was lucky, just bruising. Look I'm really sorry, but I've got someone else coming in at five. Was that all?'

'I think so,' said Capel, standing up and picking up his phone. 'Oh, erm, her agent. What was his name?'

'Norman Fox. With Casemont Lanchester. One of the older literary agencies. All wooden filing cabinets and wilting aspidistras. They're a dying breed in the trade, though they do have some more dynamic staff now.' Patel led them back to the reception. 'So nice to meet you, Capel.' She shook his hand. 'And you, Mr

Ridge.'

Ed held the door open for Capel then bounded down the stairs alongside him. 'What do you think, then, O sleuth? I suspect that this will be a three-pint problem.'

Capel smiled and shook his head. 'First find your pub.'

Ed pointed to a sign on the next building. 'The Depot. Looks a bit trendy, but this is Islington, so what can you expect? First one's on me?'

'Isn't it going to be all craft lager and wheat beer? I had a jam doughnut beer the other day in a rib restaurant. Though to be fair, that was surprisingly pleasant.'

'We'll just have to take the risk.'

By the time Ed had got a pair of beers, Capel had texted Vicky with an update and was scrolling through apps on his phone. 'Nothing decent on draft, I'm afraid,' said Ed. 'But they had cans of a decent looking IPA and it's not ridiculously cold.'

'Hmm,' said Capel. 'What did you think of Ms Patel?'

'She couldn't seem to make up her mind how close her relationship with Miss LeVine was. But her alibi sounded easy enough to check up on. What were you doing with that phone?'

'I was looking for that app you install so you can find the phone when you've lost it, though the logic of it somewhat escapes me, as when I need the app, I don't have my phone to be able to use it. It seemed sensible I should keep an eye on the phone now it's holding a recording that's technically evidence. Though I've only actually lost a phone twice.'

'You use the app on a different…' Ed sighed.

'There's really no point explaining, is there? We can do better than the built-in app, if you don't mind me using something from the old firm.'

'Please, be my guest.' Capel handed over his phone. 'Any other thoughts about the editor?'

'Professional… hang on, I need to concentrate to set this up.'

'I'll get some crisps.' Capel left Ed with the phone and headed up to the bar. He returned clutching a bulging packet. 'They didn't have any ordinary flavours. I got pheasant and thyme.'

'Tasty,' said Ed 'and there you go.' He started to hand over the phone. 'Hang on, do you want the bog-standard version or the serious one?'

'The difference being?'

'With the bog-standard one I can locate your phone. With significantly better accuracy than is available to commercial GPS, I should say. If you opt for the luxury version, I can also retrieve texts and conversations, should you wish to revisit them. Even if you delete them. And there are one or two other tasty little extras.'

'That sounds very useful, if more than a little Big Brother.'

'Don't worry, GCHQ can do it all anyway, if they get the urge. This is just a way to make the results available to you, or at least to me on your behalf.'

'Go for it.' Capel took back the phone after Ed had touched the screen a couple of times and closed down an app that promptly disappeared from the home screen. 'So how are Fliss and the kids?'

CHAPTER 8

Vicky pulled up in the Brewery cark park in Cirencester. 'Could you get the ticket?' she asked Detective Constable Yaxley. He had been assigned to accompany her in the attempt to track down the local history enthusiast, Simon Smith, and clearly resented Vicky's involvement in the Marlborough investigation. Or maybe he just didn't like female officers. He had hardly spoken on the forty-minute drive up into Gloucestershire.

'Yeah,' said Yaxley. A big man, he unfolded himself from her car like a piece of origami and lumbered over towards the pay machine.

Vicky tried to get her first questions lined up in her head. Smith lived in Marlborough, but worked as a solicitor in Cirencester. He seemed peripheral to the case, but Suki Dawson had implied that Smith had somehow managed to ruffle LeVine's feathers. At the very least, he was worth pinning down.

A tap on the window made her jump. She opened it and took the ticket Yaxley offered. 'It's free from three. Bargain.'

'Mm,' said Vicky. She checked the map on her phone. 'Smith's office is in Black Jack Street, above a bookshop. Down this way.'

'So, erm, you saw it happen,' said Yaxley. 'Saw her killed.'

'Yes, I was there,' said Vicky.

'Awesome,' said Yaxley.

'Not really.'

'Well, no, I didn't mean... Look, we weren't thrilled about you being drafted in, right? Like somehow it was saying we can't cope on our own. But I'm trying to be fair. Give you a chance.'

'Why the change of heart?'

'I reckon Alicia Crawford's jealous, because you're better looking than her. No offence. And no one wants to get on the wrong side of Alicia. But I was thinking in the car, and it's not fair, is it?'

Vicky fought down the urge to make a comment on Yaxley's thought processes or lack of them. 'That's good you want to give me a chance. I don't want any trouble, but Margaret LeVine was a nice woman, and I want to catch the bastard behind this. I've no interest in showing off.'

'I want to find him too. Ideally without winding Sergeant Crawford up. I've not been out of uniform long. I don't want to be back in it any time soon. And I'm always being compared with golden boy.'

'Sorry?' said Vicky, taking a moment to check the map again. 'Who?'

'DC Sutton. Jamie bloody "I've got a degree and don't you forget it" Sutton. Crawford thinks the sun shines out of his arse. Fast tracked, semi-pro athlete, even if it is some poncey kind of biathlon without guns, and general highflyer.'

'I know the type.' Vicky waited for a gap in the traffic and crossed.

'That's just the start – just don't ever ask him about his time with the Met. Claims he was seconded into the security services. He thinks he's practically James bloody Bond.'

Vicky snorted. 'I'll try to swerve him. Black Jack Street's just down here. Do you want to take the lead with Smith?'

'Christ, no. If there's a cock-up, I don't want to be the one who takes the blame.'

'Cheers. So, you're happy for me to get the blame?'

'No. Yes.' Yaxley sighed. 'It's complicated.'

'Welcome to the wonderful world of policing,' said Vicky. They turned into Black Jack Street. 'This is rather cute,' said Vicky. The street was narrow, little more than the width of a car, home to a continuous range of buildings in mellow Cotswold stone, from a butcher's shop down to a French restaurant. The bookshop was one of the first shops on the street – assuming there wasn't more than one bookshop – and there, to the left of it, was a smart black door with a discreet brass plate declaring it to be the home of Fosset and Sweetborough, Solicitors.

Yaxley pushed at the door, but it was locked. Vicky pressed the buzzer on the intercom below the brass plate. 'Hello? I'm DC Denning and this is DC Yaxley from the police. We'd like a word with Mr Smith.'

'Come right up.'

The door buzzed and Yaxley pushed it open. It led straight to a staircase, decorated with black and white movie posters. Yaxley held the door for Vicky, letting her take the lead.

A middle-aged woman with bright red glasses was waiting at the top of the stairs. 'Was Mr Smith expecting you?'

Vicky sucked air over her teeth. 'Not exactly. But it would be very convenient if we could see him as soon as possible. It's concerning a murder.'

The woman's eyes widened. 'I, we… could you just hang on a moment.' She disappeared behind a door, one of four on the narrow landing. Seconds later she returned. 'Please, go straight in, Mr Smith will see you now.'

Smith was seated on the far side of minimalist modern desk, featuring only a large Apple computer and a Newton's cradle desk toy. 'Hello,' he said. 'Please, take a seat.'

Vicky sat opposite and Yaxley pulled up a second chair, angled between them. He took out his notebook, pencil poised, and looked expectantly at Vicky.

No pressure then, thought Vicky. 'We're here about the death of Margaret LeVine. I believe you knew her?'

Smith opened a drawer and pulled out a well-chewed pencil. 'Yes, erm, we were both interested in local history. I live in Marlborough as well, you see. I mean, I did as well as she did, when she was alive. Sorry, I'm a bit nervous. I've never been interviewed by the police before. I'm not that sort of solicitor. Margaret and I quite often talked about history.' He bit hard enough on the end of the pencil to make an audible crunch.

Vicky frowned. She had her questions mentally lined up, but something was distracting her. There was something familiar about Smith. He was in his thirties, brown hair cut very short. Washed out green-grey eyes. Quite a big nose. It was like when you saw someone on TV who you knew had been in another programme, but you couldn't quite pin down which one it had been. She was conscious of the seconds stretching out and Yaxley, looking up curiously from his notebook at her silence.

'Did you see Miss LeVine at all on Saturday?'

asked Vicky. 'The day she died.'

'No. No, I would have remembered that.'

'Can you tell me where you were on Saturday evening, say between five and nine?'

'I, er, just a moment.' Smith turned to his computer and pulled up a diary. 'I was in a meeting all evening.'

'A meeting on a Saturday night?' said Yaxley. 'Really? I thought solicitors like you were pretty much nine to five.' His voice was flat.

'Yes,' said Smith. 'It wasn't work. Just meeting a few friends with similar interests.'

Suddenly it clicked where Vicky had seen that face before. Shit, she thought. She had to do this carefully. 'Okay, we can follow that up later. And how about Sunday morning? Where were you then?'

'Sunday?' Smith looked shifty. 'What do you mean? What's Sunday got to do with it? She was already dead by then.'

Vicky heard Yaxley shift in his seat, pulling himself more upright. At least he was with it enough to realise this question had hit a delicate spot. 'It's a simple question, Mr Smith. Where were you on Sunday morning?'

'If you must know, I was out Bath way. Doing some historical research. I can show you exactly where.' He pushed back his chair. 'I just need to get my phone from my coat.' Smith stepped around the desk. His hand was on the door handle as Vicky spoke again.

'Did you visit a Reverend Capel in Thornton Down when you were "out Bath way", Mr Smith? Did you tell Mr Capel that you were Margaret LeVine's nephew, Russell?'

Smith frowned. 'No, that's ridiculous, I, er…' The door crashed against the wall and he shot out of the room.

Vicky was already out of her chair. 'Come on then!' she shouted at Yaxley, who seemed to be having trouble deciding what to do with his notebook. Vicky rattled down the stairs after Smith, who had reached the bottom, wrenching open the street door. She saw Smith run out into Black Jack Street, straight in front of van that was inching its way down the narrow roadway. The van's bumper caught the back of Smith's leg. He stumbled, giving Vicky a chance to get close. 'Stop unless you want to be tasered,' Vicky said.

Smith froze, ignoring the gesturing of the van driver. Vicky kept her hand under her jacket as Yaxley squeezed past her and grabbed Smith.

'I don't remember a taser being authorised,' Yaxley muttered to Vicky.

'It wasn't,' Vicky whispered. 'I just wanted to slow him down.'

'Will you get out of the bloody road!' shouted the van driver.

Yaxley pushed Smith back towards the open office doorway.

'Not there,' said Smith. 'Please, not in front of my colleagues. There's a waffle place just down the road on the left.'

Vicky, hearing 'an awful place' looked puzzled for a moment until she saw the sign *He Says, She Waffles* above a low opening into a courtyard.

'Sounds a good idea,' said Yaxley, suddenly looking pleased.

Vicky bit her lip. Strictly she was not Yaxley's

superior, but he was clearly acting as if she was in charge of the operation. Any decisions were going to be down to her. 'Okay,' she said to Smith. 'But I have to warn you that if you give us any cause for concern, we will have to arrest you in a very public location.'

Smith held his hands up. 'I'm not going to be any trouble.'

Vicky raised her eyebrows, but ushered Smith into a courtyard off the street. The waffle shop was bright and colourful. Vicky ordered three coffees, hesitated and added a waffle each.

'I'll get these,' said Smith.

Again, Vicky bit her lip. She wasn't sure if this constituted accepting an inappropriate gift from a suspect – but she assured herself that she'd never had a problem with having coffee and biscuits in someone's house. Smith wasn't under arrest, he was helping the police voluntarily. How was this different? But she'd have a word with Yaxley on the way back to Marlborough about keeping quiet.

They sat at a round table, well away from any other customers. Vicky did not give Smith any time for small talk. 'So, if you aren't going to be any trouble, why did you run away from a police officer, Mr Smith? You're a solicitor. You know that that's not a good look for anyone. And why did you impersonate Miss LeVine's nephew when you visited Reverend Capel?'

Smith grimaced. 'I, er, I ran because I wasn't thinking straight. You freaked me out. But I have no idea what you mean about the nephew. It wasn't me.'

Yaxley smiled widely at the waitress who brought over the coffees. 'Thanks.'

'The waffles will just be a couple of minutes. I'll

bring them over.'

Yaxley's smiled widened more, but he waited until the waitress was out of earshot before turning back to Smith. 'Impersonating the relative of a murder victim does tend to make you a person of interest.'

'Like I said, it wasn't me. Okay? I've never heard of this Reverend Capel.'

'But we have a witness who says it was you,' said Vicky. 'He pointed you out to me in Marlborough, but you gave us the slip. Why did you do it, Mr Smith? Let's face it, you wouldn't have run from your office if it wasn't you. Just tell us what happened.'

Smith stared into his coffee for a long time. 'Look, I've just got a new car, okay? A Tesla. The roads were quiet. I wanted to see if it could really do what they say. They accelerate like a fucking rat out of a drainpipe. Sorry. So… I was driving a bit faster than I should have been. On the way to the Bath area. Quite a lot faster than I should have been. I thought…'

'You thought this was about a speeding offence? And that's why you ran?' asked Yaxley, conspicuously opening his notebook and flicking through to an empty page.

'It's stupid, I know,' said Smith. 'I panicked. But I was just exploring the area. I did not impersonate anyone.'

'We can clear this up,' said Vicky. 'Hang on.' She pulled out her phone and Facetimed Capel, but there was no reply. Vicky shook her head and sent Capel a quick text. 'I need to wait for someone to get back to me,' she said to Smith, 'but for now, tell me about your relationship with Miss LeVine. Did you get on well?'

'Look, Margaret and I were old friends. We both

had an interest in history, particularly Anglo-Saxon history of late. But she liked to tease me with little snippets that didn't give too much away when she'd found out something that she knew I'd be interested in. She could drag these things out for weeks.'

'I heard that the two of you argued recently,' said Vicky.

'I wouldn't call it arguing. It's just that she was dangling a particularly tantalising piece of information a little out of my reach. I'd call it cruel. I thought…'

The waitress came over and gave each of them a waffle with maple syrup. Vicky paused to take a bite and savour it. 'You thought?'

'Hmm? Oh, yes, Margaret had said it concerned a reeve of Bath, and that she was going to see this Capel chap. I mean, come on, a reeve of Bath? That's right up my street.'

'I thought you specialised in the history of Marlborough?' said Yaxley. 'It's not exactly local, is it, Bath?'

'Local is what you make of it, detective. Bath is about as far west as I concern myself, but Marlborough and Bath have strong historical connections. And for an Anglo-Saxon reeve I'm happy to stretch things. You don't get new information on one of those every day.'

Vicky gritted her teeth at the use of 'detective', which always felt inappropriately American. 'And a reeve is?'

'Ah, right. A reeve was the monarch's stand-in back then.'

'Like a Lord Lieutenant?' asked Yaxley. 'I've met the Lord Lieutenant of Wiltshire – a nice lady, but decidedly scary when she's doing the job.'

'Exactly,' said Smith. 'In fact, the Lords Lieutenant are direct replacements for the shire reeves – reeves for a county. Except we tend to use a contraction of the original name. A shire reeve was nothing more or less than a sheriff. Exactly the same role. The reeve in question, Alfred, was a city reeve for Bath rather than a shire reeve, but it's a similar concept. He was the local bigwig, and by repute he was extremely wealthy.'

'This is fascinating,' said Vicky, 'but it doesn't really explain what you were doing heading out in the Bath direction. Are you telling me it's a coincidence you chose to test your new car by driving in that direction?'

'I hold my hands up,' said Smith. 'Mm, this is delicious. Erm, the thing is, according to the Anglo-Saxon Chronicle, this Reeve Alfred left behind a great treasure. Anglo-Saxon treasure hordes can be absolutely magnificent. Think Sutton Hoo and all that. Worth millions, not that the money matters. Margaret hinted that she might have found some information that would lead to the horde. I was intending to visit this Reverend Capel chap, but not by impersonating Russell. Why would I do that? I was just going as my own self.'

'So, essentially you were grubbing around for treasure as soon as you heard that Miss LeVine was dead?' said Yaxley.

'I wouldn't put it like that,' said Smith. 'But yes, I did realise the timing was a little thoughtless. Only, I didn't think it would cause any offence because I didn't expect to be interviewed by the police about it. In the end, though, I decided against it. I turned back before I got there. It wasn't me your Reverend Whatsisface saw. I thought I'd leave a bit more of a decent interval after… you know… before I followed it up.'

'Okay,' said Vicky. 'Did you say what the meeting was about that you were attending when Miss LeVine was killed? Or where it was? Or who was there? I don't remember you mentioning that.'

Smith dropped his fork, which bounced off the table onto the floor. 'I'm sorry,' he said, picking it up and wiping it on his napkin. 'You surely don't think that I've anything to do with Margaret's murder?'

'We have to ask everyone,' said Yaxley. 'It's routine.'

'And it doesn't sound great, does it?' said Vicky. 'You discover that Miss LeVine has wind of some extremely valuable treasure. She could be close to finding it. Then suddenly she dies, and the next day you're driving out to Thornton Down on the trail of the goodies. It would be very convenient for you if Miss LeVine was out of the way, wouldn't it?'

'I assure you, nothing was further from my mind,' said Smith. 'And it was just a local history group committee meeting. I was there all evening. You can check with the chair, Rupert Grimes. I've got his details here.' He took out his phone, flicked through the address book and showed it to Yaxley, who scribbled in his notebook. 'There were half a dozen people who can confirm I never left the pub. The Castle and Ball on the High Street.'

'Right by where the incident happened,' said Vicky.

'I didn't know that then. But I literally never left the room. Didn't even go to the toilet. You daren't with that lot. Turn your back and someone'll stab you in it. Sorry, that's a bit tasteless.'

'Okay,' said Vicky. 'You can be sure that we will check with those who were there and the CCTV, so I'd make sure that is a totally accurate description of what happened. I'm going to have to ask you to come into the station in Marlborough and give a statement. Can you do that today?'

'Yes, of course,' said Smith. 'Anything to help.'

Vicky's phone rang. 'Hang on.' She glanced it at: Capel on Facetime. Vicky touched the screen and Capel appeared, looking vaguely doubtful as he always did on video calls. 'You okay?' she asked.

'I'm fine,' said Capel. 'Ed and I are having fun in the big bad city. How's it going?'

'I just want you to take a look at someone,' Vicky said. She flipped the view to the rear camera and held it up so Smith was on view. 'Do you recognise this man?'

'You've got him?' said Capel. 'Yes, that's my fake Levine.'

'He doesn't look entirely like your E-FIT.'

'No, the hair's too short and the face is all wrong. Sorry. I said I would be no good at it.'

'Don't worry,' said Vicky. 'See you later.' She put down the phone, took a long drink of her coffee and raised an eyebrow at Smith. 'Okay, Mr Smith, you have just been positively identified as the person who impersonated Russell Levine. Would you like to tell us about your drive on Sunday morning without the fabrication?'

Smith poked the remains of his waffle with his spoon. 'Okay, I was stupid. I thought I could bluff it out.'

'You're a solicitor, for God's sake,' said Yaxley. 'You must have known you wouldn't get away with it.'

'Like I said, I only do civil law. You know, conveyancing and such. I'm not experienced…' Smith's voice trailed off.

'Last chance, Mr Smith,' said Vicky. 'Tell us about visiting the Reverend Capel on Sunday morning.'

'Okay, yes, it was a fishing trip,' said Smith. 'Trying to get some info. I'd heard about Margaret's theory. With her out of the way, I knew that Russell would soon be sniffing after the treasure, so I wanted to get in there first. Don't get me wrong, the history is genuinely my prime interest, but if there was an Anglo-Saxon hoard to be found, I wasn't going to say "No", was I? I thought if I turned up as a complete stranger I wouldn't get anywhere, but if I pretended to be Russell this vicar would be an easy touch. Sympathetic, you know?'

'Charming,' said Vicky.

'It never occurred to me that anyone would suspect I was someone different. It's not as if I found out anything useful, anyway. And like I said, I was in the local history meeting all evening when Margaret was killed. Grimes will back me up, and the others. It wasn't me who did it.'

CHAPTER 9

'I wish I could come up to London with you,' said Capel next morning, waving a piece of toast at a pile of papers. 'Hitting the big city with Ed has given me a taste for the high life. But I've got a Standing Committee meeting to go through the latest set of bright ideas from the bishop before we have to put them to the PCC. I love the bish dearly, and there's no doubt the diocese did need a shakeup, but sometimes I think that she is too focused on making a difference and not enough on achieving stability.'

'That's funny, coming from you,' said Vicky. 'It's probably just as well you aren't coming with me, though. Chief Inspector Morley is used to you, but I get the impression that some of the Marlborough lot aren't totally impressed with your involvement. I'm meeting up with one of their DCs at Swindon station to go and interview Miss LeVine's agent. Inevitably, the agency's in London.' She sighed. 'There's too much travel involved in this case.'

'Don't knock it,' said Capel. 'It gets you out and about. You're not saddled with that Yaxley again, are you? You didn't seem impressed last night.'

'No, it's the other one. Erm...' she flipped open her notebook. 'Jamie Sutton. Sergeant Crawford seemed to pick up that Yaxley and I didn't hit it off. Mind you, if Yaxley is right, this Sutton is full of himself.'

'Good luck with him, then. You'd better get on, though – I don't suppose Marlborough has many detective constables and you seem to be getting through them rather quickly.'

Vicky curled her lip. 'Hilarious.'

'So, do you think the agent will know anything useful?'

'It's possible. But I was also wondering about Suki Dawson's mystery visitor. It's a longshot, but you told me that Margaret mentioned that her agent was quite involved in the literary festival. What if our Mr Fox…'

'Was being a bit foxy on the side?'

'Exactly. It's worth checking his whereabouts.'

~

'I wouldn't say he's sexist, exactly, but Yaxley is of the opinion that women are best suited to being in uniform.'

Vicky laughed. 'I got that impression. Not your viewpoint, though, DC Sutton?'

'Jamie, please. Look, we're policing in the twenty-first century, not the dark ages.'

'Tell me about it.'

'So, how did you end up engaged to a vicar? You don't strike me as vicar's wife material. No offence.'

Vicky smiled. 'That's becoming a very familiar phrase. Capel – my fiancé – gets it every time someone swears in front of him, but it looks like it's catching. In this case I don't take offence at all. I'm not sure that I am cut out to be a traditional vicar's wife. But I *am* sure that I'm engaged, which will lead to me becoming a vicar's wife. It's hard to explain. But Capel's not that kind of vicar, and the Church of England isn't as conservative as it used to be. His bishop's a woman, for example.'

'He's a lucky vicar.'

Vicky shook her head. 'Focus, DC Sutton. Jamie. What do we know about the fantastic Mr Fox?'

'Yes, ma'am. I can see you're destined for higher things – ordering people around comes naturally.' Sutton ducked as Vicky swiped at him with her bag. 'Norman Fox. You don't get many Normans these days, do you? He's been Margaret LeVine's agent for fifteen years. A regular visitor to Marlborough – he helped her set up the festival. Really hands on.'

'I thought the festival had been running longer than that?'

'It started a couple of years earlier, but it only really took off when LeVine and Fox got involved.'

Vicky glanced up at the indicator board on the tube. 'Next stop is us.'

Sutton checked his phone. 'We're a good half hour early. Do you fancy a coffee first? No point in getting there before we're expected.'

'Why not.'

The October sunlight was thin, but the London street they emerged into was bustling. 'There's a place over there,' said Sutton, pointing across the road to a small independent café.

'Looks great,' said Vicky.

~

'I think that's about it,' said Capel. He glanced at the others, who nodded in unison. Diana Tarlton, the churchwarden sighed. 'It's going to be easier when we get another warden. Am I right in thinking Simon can start contributing before he's elected at the next

APCM?'

'I don't want to be pernickety, Diana.' Peter Finch scratched his large nose. 'But the wardens are not elected by the APCM.'

Sensing the potential for a lengthy dispute on something that did not matter in the least, Capel stood up, hoping to encourage the others to get moving. 'Yes,' he said, 'Simon can attend meetings and undertake some duties before his election. Technically Peter is right. The churchwardens are elected by the whole parish – anyone who lives in the parish, whether or not they are churchgoers, can attend and vote. Which means there is a separate Parish Meeting, usually immediately before the Annual Parochial Church Meeting. The APCM *is* only for those on the electoral roll.'

'Fair enough,' said Tarlton. 'And am I also right in thinking that strictly speaking the Standing Committee is inquorate?'

Capel sighed. Diana Tarlton was not the kind of person to be left on the back foot. She had to reassert her authority with a technicality. 'Yes.'

'Bloody bureaucracy,' muttered Finch.

'The rules and regulations of the Church of England, as you are aware, can be fairly labyrinthine. As well as the PCC, we are legally obliged to have a Standing Committee, which should consist of the priest, the wardens and at least two other members of the PCC. But on the plus side, the C of E is quite good at pragmatism. We get by.'

The doorbell rang, cutting through Tarlton's reply. 'Sorry,' said Capel. 'I'd better get that.'

He opened the door to find Roland Mclean standing with his arms folded on the step.

'Roland, what a nice surprise.'

'You almost sounded as if you meant that.'

'Have you time for a pub lunch? I need an excuse to winkle out some committee members.'

'Why not,' said Mclean. 'I can't resist a good lunchtime pint, especially if you're buying.'

Capel refrained from pointing out that Mclean's salary was at least four times his stipend. 'Of course.' He turned back into the house. 'Diana? Peter? I'm afraid I'm going to have to chuck you out. My next appointment's here.'

Finch emerged into the hall. 'Hmm,' he said to Mclean.

'Good morning,' said Mclean. He glanced at his watch. 'Afternoon, I mean.'

'Have we met?' asked Tarlton as she came out of Capel's study. 'I'm Diana Tarlton.'

'A pleasure,' said Mclean. 'Roland Mclean. County pathologist and friend of the family.'

'A pathologist?' said Tarlton. 'How fascinating.'

'Not now, woman,' said Finch. 'You can see he wants rid of us.'

Five minutes later, Capel led Mclean across to the Forge, Thornton Down's sole pub. Mclean eyed up the row of beer engines. 'What do you recommend? They've changed the beers since I was last in here.'

'Moles is nice and light for lunchtime.'

'And cheap,' Mclean noted. 'But that's fine.'

They ordered food and headed over to a table by the open fire. 'Misplaced my goddaughter today?'

'She's up in London with another man.'

Mclean shook his head. 'I did warn her the gloss would fade. I just didn't expect it would be this quick. Gone for a younger model, has she?'

'I don't know how old he is, we've never met. It's a police colleague.'

'I recommend that you do meet him. Suss out the opposition.'

Capel snorted. 'Vicky and I are engaged, Roland. He's her colleague. Nothing more to say. So, have you got some news for us? About Margaret LeVine.'

'The formal report will be with the police tomorrow, but I thought I'd give you the edited highlights.' He paused as a waitress brought over a pair of bowls of chilli nachos. 'Mm, that looks good. Thanks.' Mclean picked up his fork and pointed it at Capel. 'If you remember, we were all a wee bit stumped by the mystery of the disappearing weapon.'

'All too well,' said Capel.

'I've news,' said Mclean.

~

'That was nice, thanks,' said Sutton.

'It was. Good idea. What number's the agency?'

'Erm, two seven seven. Should be those offices over there.' He pointed to a dingy-looking Victorian building that might have been a bank at one point. They crossed the street. Closer up, the building seemed in better repair. An incongruously modern plaque by the door proclaimed this to be the offices of Casemont Lanchester.

The receptionist pointed them to a waiting area. 'Did you check this lot out?' asked Vicky.

'No. Sorry. I had a Netflix evening last night.'

'Netflix and chill?'

Sutton sniffed. 'Netflix and a pizza. On my own. It's just me. Alone. With the pizza and the TV.'

'Sad case,' said Vicky. 'If you'd bothered to do some research, you'd have discovered that Casemont Lanchester is a rarity in being both an actors' agency and a literary agency. It's been the luvvies' best friend since 1924. Got some quite impressive clients.'

'I wonder…' Sutton broke off as a corpulent man with an Einstein-like shock of white hair approached.

'You are the police? I am Norman Fox. I believe you wish to speak with me.'

'Yes,' said Vicky, standing up. 'Is there somewhere we can talk privately?'

Fox pointed to a pair of double doors across the foyer, which led into a dark panelled meeting room. When they were seated around a table that could easily have accommodated twenty, Fox ran his fingers through his hair. 'With what, precisely, do you believe I can help you?'

'Margaret LeVine,' said Vicky. 'As you know, we are investigating her death. When did you last see her?'

Fox pulled a slim, leather-bound diary from his pocket and flicked through the pages. 'That would be the Friday before last. I met Margaret in Marlborough to talk a few things through.' He replaced the diary and patted his jacket as if to bed it in.

Vicky nodded. 'But you weren't in Marlborough the night that Margaret died? Last Saturday, the seventeenth.'

Fox laboriously pulled his diary out again. 'No. I was in town for an event at BAFTA. I only represent authors, but here at Casemont Lanchester we have a considerable stable of highly respected actors on our books. My colleagues inform me that they are a nightmare to deal with, but they do have the best parties.'

'How well did you know Miss LeVine?' asked Sutton.

'She was a good, steady client – and a friend. She was midrange, nothing too flashy, but a reliable earner. You need a mix of talent in my business. The rising stars can be like fireworks, shining bright but burning out equally quickly. A solid, steady performer provides useful ballast.'

'Was she happy with her publisher?' asked Vicky.

'Ah,' said Fox. 'You may well ask. The short answer is no. They used to have an excellent publicist there, but she left for one of their bigger rivals. Since then, Margaret felt that her books were not getting enough exposure. To be fair, no author does think their books get the publicity they deserve, but in this case the viewpoint was justified. We were in active discussion with a number of other publishers.'

'Would her editor at Encaustic know about this?' asked Vicky.

'Not officially. But it's hard to keep secrets in this business. I would be surprised if Ms Patel didn't know something was afoot.'

'Which wouldn't please her?' said Sutton.

'Obviously not. But it happens. It would be unlikely to turn her murderous overnight.'

Sutton nodded as Vicky scribbled in her notebook. 'And you were personally involved in the literary festival?'

'Oh, yes, for many years. Obviously, as an agency we support festivals in general – they provide a good opportunity to get our clients' books in front of the audience at relatively little cost. But Marlborough was something of a labour of love for Margaret – Miss

LeVine – and I was happy to spend a considerable amount of my spare time helping her with it. I don't have a family. It was a diversion. I shall miss it – and her. She was good company.'

'You won't be continuing to be involved with the festival?' asked Vicky. 'I got the impression that Suki Dawson intends to keep it alive.'

'Pah,' said Fox.

It occurred to Vicky that this was a sound she had only ever read in books, never heard from a real person. Fox seemed determined to make himself a caricature of an old school literary agent. She realised Fox had been speaking. 'Sorry?'

'Mizz Dawson is no Margaret LeVine. I have no interest in helping her to succeed with her ridiculous machinations.'

'Sorry,' said Sutton, 'are you suggesting that Suki Dawson could have been responsible for Margaret LeVine's death in some way?'

'Not at all,' said Fox. 'The woman hasn't got the brains for it. But there is no doubt that she is salivating at the opportunity to get her clammy paws on Margaret's festival. I can't imagine that Mrs Dawson was behind the death, but she is just the sort of opportunist to make the most of it, if she got the chance.'

'And just to be clear, you have never been to Mrs Dawson's house?' asked Vicky.

'Thankfully, no. I can imagine unaided just how tasteless it would be. Tacky porcelain figurines, at the very least, I suspect.'

'Is there anyone you can think of who would have both the ability and the inclination to kill Miss LeVine?' asked Sutton.

'Hmm.' Fox stared up at the ceiling. Sutton raised his eyebrows at Vicky. 'If you were asking my colleagues who deal with actors, they would have no problem finding a good number with the inclination to kill their rivals, but few with the ability. In my world, things are largely more refined. Of course, the crime writers spend their time endlessly plotting a character's demise, but they rarely have the personality to put their imaginings into practice. So, I'm afraid I can't provide you with a list of potential suspects. I can, however, tell you who did it.'

CHAPTER 10

From the pick-up point below Bath station, Capel watched Vicky's train pull up on the high-level platform. He switched the taxi's engine on to get some warmth into the car before she emerged into the darkness.

'The Gainsborough Hotel, please.'

Capel jumped. He had been focused on watching the train and hadn't seen the elderly lady approach from the station's back entrance. She had an American accent and was wheeling an extremely large aluminium case.

'I'm sorry,' said Capel, 'this isn't a taxi anymore.'

'It's not that late,' said the woman. 'You can take a fare, surely?'

'No, I don't mean I'm off duty, it's a private car.' Capel sighed. 'I'm not a taxi driver, I'm a vicar. A pastor. The taxi rank is round the front of the station.'

'Round…?'

Capel paused for a moment and then smiled. 'Please, let me help.' He turned off the engine and got out of the car. 'This way. Would you like a hand with your bag?'

'Thank you very much.'

Capel led the woman through the long, arched tunnel under the station to the taxi rank at the front of the building. 'Here you go.'

'Thank you, you are very kind. Though *your* cab looks much nicer.'

Capel waved and jogged back through the tunnel to find Vicky leaning against the side of the taxi.

'Sorry, just dealing with another fare,' he said. 'You look worn out.'

'Home, driver.'

'No problem. I've got a bit of news for you.'

'Me too. You go first.'

'No, really, after you,' said Capel.

'It seems the agent was not Suki Dawson's mystery visitor. He was far too old, and he can't stand Suki. But he did claim to know who killed Margaret.'

'That's impressive.'

'Hmm. Fox is convinced that the killer was another author, Cherie Taylor. Apparently, she had tried to get on Fox's books, but he didn't want to represent a rival of Miss LeVine's, and he's convinced that Ms Taylor was so desperate to be represented by him that she would happily murder her rival to get access to the fantastic Mr Fox.'

'You've called him that already today, haven't you? The way you came out with the fantastic Mr Fox was way too slick.'

'Yes, alright, you know me too well. But as far as I can see, Fox's revelation tells us more about his self-importance than it does about a realistic suspect. I'm not saying Cherie Taylor is innocent – but I don't think we can give any weight to Fox's claim.'

'There was the review,' said Capel.

'Review?'

'Sorry, I forgot. Maneet Patel had said to check out Margaret's review in the Sunday Times of Taylor's last book. It's apparently a bit of a hatchet job.'

'Forgot? Bloody hell, send an amateur to do a professional's job.'

'Sorry.' Capel pulled out into the early evening traffic.

Vicky was typing into her phone. After a minute or two she snorted. 'Oh, wow.'

'Not a glowing review, then?'

'Listen to this. "Review by Margaret LeVine of Cherie Taylor's *Doctor Dee*. The Tudor scholar and magician John Dee has proved to be a veritable candle flame to a moth for many a writer of historical fiction, especially those with a penchant for a combination of tawdry romance with clichéd plots and two-dimensional characters. Taylor's latest doorstop of a book does not disappoint in this regard. Admittedly, there is a degree of depth in her version of Edward Kelley, the roguish occultist who seems to have had a parasitic relationship with Dee, but his portrayal stands out in what is otherwise a miserable cast of stock characters. Taylor's John Dee comes across as more Tweedle Dum than Tweedle Dee. From anachronistic language to a total lack of understanding of the Elizabethan psyche, Taylor demonstrates again and again that she is out of her depth. For a period well-supplied with excellent historical novels, this is a totally unnecessary addition." I can't see that would have made Margaret one of Cherie Taylor's favourite people.'

'Hmm,' said Capel. 'You'd expect that Taylor would be looking for a chance to trash Margaret's career in revenge, but it still seems flimsy as a motive for murder.'

'We also need to consider that Fox told us that Margaret was thinking of changing publishers, so your friend Maneet, his editor, might not have been too pleased with Margaret either.'

'Perhaps. But that also sounds a stretch as a motive for murder. Ms Patel did tell me a fib if what

Fox said is true – she claimed Margaret had no interest in leaving the publisher – but killing her still sounds an excessive reaction. Did you check out their alibis?'

'Not yet, Inspector Capel. It's on my list. Well, the editor is anyhow. We haven't managed to contact Cherie Taylor, but we've tried several times.'

'Hmm. And how did you get on with Yaxley's replacement? Was he any better?'

'Oh, yes, Jamie was much better. Very much better.'

'Jamie, is it? Very much better? Should I be jealous?'

'Don't be silly. I don't deny he's easy on the eye and easy to talk to, and good to work with. And intelligent and funny. But it's purely business.'

'If you say so. Meanwhile, I had lunch with the godfather from hell, and he's got an idea for the murder weapon.'

'Which is what?'

'Something of a mystery. He wants to demonstrate. I left him back at the vicarage. I hope it was safe to leave him in the same room as my best port.'

~

'Good evening.' Roland Mclean lifted a glass in welcome as Capel and Vicky came into the room.

Capel looked closer at the brownish-red liquid in the glass and sighed. 'You found the port, then?'

'Excellent thirty-year-old tawny. Thank you.'

'So how was it done?' asked Vicky.

Mclean closed his eyes for a moment and took

another sip of the port. 'Let's see if we can come up with a theory.' He put down his glass and pulled an object in an evidence bag from his briefcase, handing it to Vicky. 'Recognise this, Vic?'

'It's one of the pencils they were giving out at the Mop fair.'

'It is, well done.'

'But you said they couldn't have been the weapon. They're too blunt, they're the wrong shape and the wood would have splintered,' said Capel.

'All correct,' said Maclean. 'Yet I am convinced that the particular pencil that Vic is holding is part of the murder weapon. It was a close thing – we nearly didn't find it. The forensics team was just about to bin a whole stack of them. Six hundred and forty-three to be precise. Which you may be fascinated to know is a prime number, though that isn't at all relevant. My assistant and I have looked at every one of them, and that one stood out.'

Capel crossed the room to a bookshelf and picked up the pencil that Maclean had given him a few days earlier. He held it up, alongside the pencil that Vicky was holding inside the plastic bag. 'The pencil itself is pretty much the same. There's some damage to the end. though: it looks a bit crumbly.'

'But the feathers are different,' said Vicky. 'They're the same colour as the other one, but they're more precisely arranged here. It's almost like the fletching on an arrow, but it's too short. More like a crossbow bolt.'

Maclean nodded. 'Good. Well done.'

Capel shook his head. 'But you said the pencil couldn't have caused that wound.'

'That's right. A crossbow would reduce the stress

at the point of firing when compared with being shot from a gun, but the end of a sharpened pencil would not have survived the impact or been able to make that wound and it would have been entirely the wrong shape. Anyway, this pencil wasn't sharpened.'

'So, there was something on the end,' said Vicky. 'Some kind of tip that has since vanished.'

'Precisely,' said Roland.

'When I saw it happen,' said Capel, 'I thought there was something shiny in the wound. Not a pencil with feathers on.'

'I imagine the pencil had fallen away by then. You were seeing the tip, as Vic called it.'

'So, I was sort of right all along?' said Capel. 'Not an ice bullet, but an ice tip to a crossbow bolt.'

'Ice wouldn't do the job,' said Maclean. 'It just isn't hard enough. Typically, ice is around 1.5 on the Moh scale. That puts it between talc and gypsum. An ice head for the bolt, shaped like a blade, would break on impact without penetrating the victim's clothing.'

'I'm sure I saw something on a documentary once,' said Vicky. 'Doesn't ice get harder as you make it colder?'

'Now we're getting somewhere,' said Maclean. 'Cool an ice arrowhead down to minus 70 – easy enough to do with liquid nitrogen – and it reaches 6 on the Moh scale. That's harder than a typical knife blade.'

'Like I said, I was nearly right,' said Capel.

'There's still one problem, though,' said Maclean. 'Supercooled ice would take even longer to disperse than the ordinary stuff. And the wound was nowhere near wet enough to be the location of an ice melt. The clue is that word "wet", if it helps.'

'I give up,' said Vicky. 'Put us out of our misery.'

Maclean looked at Capel, who shrugged and nodded.

'You have presumably heard of dry ice.'

'Solid carbon dioxide,' said Capel.

'Precisely. It's slightly harder than ice without being supercooled, but take it down to liquid nitrogen temperatures and again we're up to a Moh scale of 6. It doesn't leave any liquid residue behind – it sublimes straight to gas, and it would disappear a lot quicker when exposed to body heat when compared with water ice. To put the icing on the cake, as it were, it would also produce the kind of crumbled residue at the end of the pencil we see here. Voilà. Ingenious.'

'Would that mean the killer has to be a scientist?'

'Not necessarily. They'd have to be a good shot with a crossbow and have access to liquid nitrogen, but that's not as difficult as you might think. Most doctors' surgeries have it as a matter of course. And chefs use liquid nitrogen these days to make fancy frozen desserts. The rest, anyone could have found out on the internet.'

'Chefs?' said Vicky.

Capel frowned. 'We've not come across a chef.'

'No, but Russell Levine is apparently part owner of a chichi eatery in Hungerford. I think we need to have another word with the doting nephew.'

CHAPTER 11

Vicky stared at Inspector Davis. She couldn't remember ever seeing someone's face such a dark shade of red as the inspector's when he slammed open the main office door and stamped into the morning briefing at Marlborough Police Station.

'Let's get this straight. Russell Levine is the nephew of the victim, and as we all know, the most likely suspects in a homicide, unless someone else is found with the body, are members of the family. What's more, we now discover that the murder weapon was something that implied the perpetrator had access to liquid nitrogen, which brings Levine firmly into the frame. And then we find out that Levine has yet to be interviewed, five days after the incident? I know that was high on the action list. Crawford?'

'DC Yaxley was tasked with it, boss.'

Inspector Davis did not look impressed. 'Yaxley?'

'I, er, I thought that it was on Denning's list. I'm sorry. I got confused. She talked about Levine having met with her boyfriend and I lost track of the fact that we hadn't actually interviewed him. It slipped my mind.'

'That's why we have the system, Yaxley. You have to look at it. When it's intelligent enough to check itself and do the interviews for us, we can dispose of fucking timewasters like yourself. Right. Sutton and Denning – interview the man today. Yaxley, my office at 2pm.'

~

'She did? Thanks.' Vicky slipped her phone back in her pocket and made a note. 'It looks like the editor, Maneet Patel, is in the clear. According to the vet, she was with him far too late to have made it out to Marlborough in time. She was always a longshot.'

'But you thought you'd better check her off the list before you faced the wrath of Davis?' asked Sutton. He pulled the car to a stop at traffic lights and grinned at Vicky.

'I admit, this morning's bollocking helped concentrate the mind and ensure I didn't miss a follow-up,' said Vicky. 'On a scale of one to ten, how much shit is Yaxley in? I know how my DCI would deal with it, but I don't know if Inspector Davis is more a "one of the lads" kind of guvnor, if you know what I mean.'

'It's a twelve,' said Sutton. 'He'll come down like the proverbial. Seriously, Yaxley's going to be back in uniform tomorrow. If he's lucky.'

'Best not to get on the wrong side of Davis, then?'

'I wouldn't recommend it.' Sutton turned the car right by the Bear, Hungerford's old coaching inn, and into a road that was slow-moving with traffic. 'This is the High Street. How far up is this caff?'

'Health food haven, please. Just past the town hall,' said Vicky, peering at her phone. 'There's a car park down this side street.'

Levine's café was very modern – bright, lots of wood and tiles and blackboards, and cheerful comments like 'No excuse – just juice!' hand painted on the walls. Though Vicky's natural inclination was to take the lead, she let Sutton approach the server.

'We're here to see Mr Levine,' said Sutton, flashing his warrant card. 'He's expecting us.'

They were shown into a crowded back office. Levine was hurriedly moving piles of paperwork to clear space on a pair of small visitors' chairs. 'Sorry, sorry,' he said as they squeezed past a half-open filing cabinet. 'Life is too short for filing.'

'You could paint that on the wall,' Vicky muttered.

'Sorry?'

Vicky put on her best smile. 'Nothing, Mr Levine. We need to check a few things with you. I'm sorry we've been so slow to get in touch. There was some administrative confusion.'

'We just need to clarify a few details, really,' said Sutton. 'Can we start with the day itself. Where were you between five pm and nine pm on the evening of Saturday the seventeenth of October?'

Levine slumped into the chair behind his desk and stroked his beard. 'Where I should have been was with Aunt Margaret. She was meeting up with a vicar and his fiancée…' He paused a moment and looked straight at Vicky. 'Was it you? Were you there?'

Vicky nodded. 'Yes, I'm sorry. It was me.'

'So, what happened?' asked Sutton. 'Why didn't you make it?'

'Stupid work stuff. I was here. Trying to get the VAT sorted out. Then the computer – I use an online accounting package – the computer started messing me about. I was here from just after lunch through to at least eight in the evening. By the time I got back to Marlborough – it's about a twenty-minute drive down the A4 from here – and got changed I thought I'd call it a day. I did text Aunt Margaret at maybe five in the afternoon to tell her I was unlikely to make it and said to carry on without me.'

'Have you got your phone with you?' said Vicky.

Levine frowned. 'Yes, I suppose… hang on.' He checked his jacket pockets, then shifted several piles of paper on the desk before uncovering a battered phone. He flipped through to the texts and handed the phone to Vicky. 'There. It was actually quarter past five when I messaged her.'

'Thanks,' said Vicky.

'Can anyone verify your whereabouts that evening?' asked Sutton.

'For the first part of the time, yes. There were staff around until six, but after that I was on my own.'

'Does your café use liquid nitrogen?' asked Vicky. Sutton, who was looking down at his notebook, looked quickly up at Vicky, but said nothing.

'No, we don't do anything as Heston Blumenthal as that. Simple, organic, good food – that's our motto.'

'But you presumably could get hold of some liquid nitrogen if you needed it?'

'Yes, sure. There are specialist catering suppliers.' Levine frowned. 'Do you need some for something? I've never ordered it myself, but I'm sure I can find a contact.'

'No, sorry,' said Vicky, 'that's fine. When you saw Reverend Capel, you asked about Miss LeVine's research and asked if Capel could take you around the sites they had discussed. Why was that?'

'I, er, I was trying to take more interest in Aunt Margaret's work in the last few months and I'd been helping her with the research. It got me interested in Anglo Saxon history and I felt that it would be a shame for her work to have been in vain. I don't know… I thought I might be able to finish her new book.'

'You?' asked Sutton. 'Are you really suggesting you intend to become a historical fiction author?'

'I am a writer already,' said Levine stiffly, sitting more upright. 'My poetry has been published in several periodicals.'

'It's very different, though, isn't it?' said Sutton. 'I mean, historical fiction involves a lot of getting your hands dirty. In-depth research. Poetry's all in your head.'

'I don't deny that it's a totally different discipline. But it's what I thought I might do. I was close to my aunt. It would be a fitting memorial.'

'Nothing to do with the possibility of finding some Anglo-Saxon treasure?'

'Of course it occurred to me that digging up the hoard would be a pleasant bonus. I'm not claiming to be a saint. But, no, it wasn't foremost in my mind.'

'Come on, Mr Levine,' said Sutton, 'this is bullshit. You wanted to get your snout in the trough, didn't you?'

'I, I don't really know what you…'

'Thanks very much,' said Vicky. 'We'll get back to you if there's anything more.' She hustled Sutton out of the café and set off towards the car at a fast pace.

Sutton hurried to catch her up. 'I'm sorry, have I done something wrong?'

'It was a bit heavy handed, don't you think? He's just lost his auntie. I know he's a suspect, but you made him seem like a money-grubbing opportunist.'

'He may be exactly that,' said Sutton. 'But I really didn't mean to be hard on him. Are you in a hurry? Perhaps we could have a drink and talk about it.' He touched her arm. 'I'd like to get to know you a bit better.'

'I'm engaged, Jamie.'

'No, oh God, I didn't… I just meant if we're working together, it's a good idea to have a feel how each other ticks, that's all. Nothing personal. Not that you're not attractive… stop digging, Jamie.'

Vicky smiled. 'I suppose a quick drink wouldn't be the end of the world. Coffee, though. Nothing alcoholic.'

Sutton smiled back. 'As if I meant anything else. We're on duty, right?'

Seated in the coffee shop across the high street five minutes later, Vicky took a sip of her latte and looked straight into Sutton's eyes without speaking.

'Good interrogation technique,' said Sutton after a few seconds. 'So, you were really there when it happened?'

'Yes,' said Vicky. 'It was horrible. I could see her, but I couldn't do anything about it because the ride pinned you in place. It took all I could do just to move my arm enough to put a call in. Weren't you at the Mop?'

Sutton shook his head. 'Not my kind of thing. I like to get out of town when the Mops are on. I had an Indian down at the Palm on the Hungerford road. Have you been there? It's a great place, even though the décor's a bit over the top. We drove past in on the way here.'

'No, I haven't,' said Vicky. 'Remember, I'm not from round here.'

'Of course, sorry. It must be strange, being seconded to another station.'

'I'm used to moving around. I was originally based

in Glastonbury, but I moved over to Bath after I met Capel.'

'Ah, yes, the mysterious vicar.'

'Nothing mysterious about him.'

'I always wanted to go to Glastonbury. The festival, I mean.'

Vicky took a bite from the brownie Sutton had provided with the coffees. 'I did one festival duty. To be honest, it was no fun. Those toilets…'

'Fair point. I suppose it's different for the workers.'

'Tell me about it.' Vicky glanced at her phone. 'Look at the time. We've got a briefing back in Marlborough. You can point out this Palm place on the way.'

Sutton smiled. 'I see my irresistible charm is working again.'

~

'Right.' Inspector Davis pawed at his iPad. 'Crawford, this thing isn't connecting.'

Sergeant Crawford glanced at the large screen TV behind Davis which was entirely blank. 'Binns?'

A uniformed officer looked up from her notebook. 'Yes, Sarge.' She took the iPad off Davis, who looked deeply embarrassed, flicked at the controls and moments later the screen was mirrored on the TV.

'Right,' said Davis again. 'Quick summary of the position on our persons of interest.' He touched Russell Levine's name, producing a diagram on screen linking Russell to the others in the case. 'Start with Levine, Crawford.'

'Denning?' said Crawford.

'Erm, we've just got back from interviewing him,' said Vicky, glancing at her notebook. 'He had witnesses who put him in Hungerford until 6pm…' she glanced at Sutton.

'Just waiting on confirmation,' Sutton said.

'After that, he claims to have been alone at his place of work in Hungerford until well after the crime was committed. If he's lying, there would have been time to have got to Marlborough. And he claims not to have had anything to do with liquid nitrogen – Dr Mclean tells us that is likely to have been involved in making the weapon. There aren't many companies that supply liquid nitrogen to caterers. We're following them up.'

Sutton nodded.

'Good,' said Crawford. 'Check traffic cameras and any ANPR on the A4. Who was on town centre CCTV?'

There was a silence as the other officers glanced at each other, then looked down at their paperwork like schoolchildren trying not to be picked to answer a question.

'Well?' said Crawford.

'Erm.' It was a male plain clothes officer that Vicky didn't know. 'DC Yaxley was supposed to be doing it, but I don't think…'

'For Christ's sake!' Davis slammed his iPad down on the table. 'Are you honestly telling me that at this stage of the game no one has checked CCTV from the bloody High Street? Why wasn't this flagged for action?'

'It was flagged. Yaxley, okay boss? He's off sick at the moment.' said Crawford. 'Before digging out his uniform. We can postmortem this later. Who'd like to volunteer to check it out now?'

'I'll do it,' said Sutton.

'Brown nose,' Vicky whispered to him.

'Excellent,' said Crawford. 'Sutton and Denning will do it straight after the briefing.'

'No, I wasn't…' Vicky let her voice trail off as Davis stared coldly at her.

'Right,' said Davis. 'Next, this solicitor historian who pretended to be Levine.'

'Smith, Simon Smith,' said Crawford.

'I interviewed him with Yaxley,' said Vicky. 'Smith was in a local history group committee meeting in the Castle and Ball. I've checked with others present – he was in full sight at the exact time Miss LeVine was killed. They went out to the front of the hotel when they heard the sirens – Smith was still with them at that point.'

'Thank you, DC Denning,' said Davis. 'How about the other writer?' He fiddled with the iPad. 'Cherie something. Cherie Taylor?'

'I've been on it, guv,' said Crawford. 'The DC assigned couldn't pin her down.'

'Yaxley again?' growled Davis.

'It was, but anyone would have had a problem,' said Crawford. 'She's bloody elusive. Never at home: I've been playing email tag with her agent and I've left a pile of messages. No one's sure where she is.'

'Well, it's time to get sure,' said Davis. 'Make it a priority. Who else have we got?'

Crawford glanced at her notebook. 'LeVine's editor, Maneet Patel has a solid alibi. What about the other festival woman, Suki Dawson?'

'She did tell us a lie initially,' said Vicky, 'but that

seemed to be to cover up an extra-marital affair. She's not eliminated yet, though.'

'Keep an eye on her,' said Davis. 'Crawford, get someone digging deeper with that one.'

'Yes, sir. And then there's LeVine's agent, Norman Fox. He was allegedly at a BAFTA event in London, but I've been having trouble getting that confirmed. I'm expecting a call from an administrator there this morning.'

'Okay, anything else? Anyone?'

~

'Thanks for the offering to stay late to help,' said Sutton as they headed back to their desks a few minutes later.

'I didn't,' said Vicky.

'I know.' Sutton grinned. 'I think it's what they call karma.' He ducked as Vicky threw a notepad at him.

'Why were you so eager to do it?' Vicky asked, pulling up the first of the feeds on her screen. 'No one wants to do CCTV. It's so boring.'

'Thinking ahead, it is,' said Sutton in a Yoda voice. 'The force is strong with a young Jedi who wisely choosing is.'

'Bollocks to that,' said Vicky. 'I was due off shift by now.'

'Look, you know what it's like. Usually checking CCTV means hours of watching nothing in the hope of catching someone out. But we know exactly when the crime was committed. So, we only have to watch from maybe an hour before. It's the easiest CCTV job you could possibly have. And then the next time someone has to trawl through a whole day's video…'

'It's not you that gets landed with it.'

'Learning, you are, young Jedi. Which feed are you looking at?'

'First one on the list. From outside Waitrose.'

'Okay, I'll take the next two and the Lloyds Bank one. Could you do the ones from further along the high street?'

'Yep, sure.'

They stared at the screens in silence for a few minutes.

'Did you have anything planned tonight, then?' asked Sutton.

'No, I just fancied a quiet night in with Capel. We… oh.'

'Oh?' Sutton paused the video he was watching and came round to look at Vicky's screen. 'That's you, isn't it? Not your best side, perhaps.'

'Piss off,' said Vicky. 'Yes, that's me, but I mean her.' She pointed to a woman. 'Right by Margaret LeVine. Hang on, I'll zoom in.' She outlined a section with the mouse and tapped the keyboard. 'A shame it's never as clear as it is when they do this on TV. But that's definitely Suki Dawson. Who told us that she was at home all evening. We've already established she wasn't alone like she said she was, but this is stretching things a lot further. It clearly wasn't the only lie she told. Dawson was due another visit, but this makes it a higher priority. Have you spotted anyone yet?'

Sutton shook his head. 'All clear so far. Should we pop over and see her now? I can finish off the videos afterwards. You can get off back to Bath and enjoy your quiet night in.'

'Are you sure, Jamie?'

'What can I say? I'm a natural gentleman.'

~

The houses on the green were set far enough back from the main road to lie beyond the reach of the streetlights. Most were brightly lit, but the Dawson house seemed entirely in darkness. Vicky pressed the doorbell. They stood for what seemed an age, though it was probably only half a minute before Sutton rapped on the door. Still no response.

Vicky pulled out her phone and flicked through in her notebook to where she'd jotted down Suki Dawson's number. She dialled, but the phone went straight to voicemail.

'Well?' said Sutton.

'Ssh, I'm listening to the message.'

Dawson's voicemail sounded irritatingly perky. 'Hi, you've reached Suki Dawson's voicemail, which means I can't get speak to you right now. Leave a message and I will get back to you as soon as I can. If I like the sound of you.'

'Hello, Ms Dawson, it's Detective Constable Denning here. We need to see you with some urgency. Could you give me a call back on this number when you get this message, please.'

'Looks like you might as well go home, then,' said Sutton.

'Are you sure? I can still go through the CCTV with you.'

'I've no one to go back home to. Drop me off at the station, then go and make your vicar happy.'

~

'What time do you call this,' Capel shouted from the kitchen as Vicky let herself in.

'Erm, about quarter to nine?'

'Exactly,' said Capel. 'You said you wouldn't be late.'

'I'm not that late. I was landed with some CCTV checking, then tried to see Suki Dawson again, but she wasn't in. You know what it's like with this job.'

'I do know, but I don't have to like it.'

CHAPTER 12

'You're not still grumpy?' said Vicky, draining the last of her morning coffee. 'I know I was later than I said I'd be, but I told you: some things came up. I had to look into them.'

'I'm fine,' said Capel. He glanced at his watch. 'What time's Margaret's nephew supposed to be here?'

'Eleven. Ten minutes yet.' Vicky took out her notebook and flicked through it. 'I've been wondering, did you ever get that notebook back?'

'Sorry?' Capel was fiddling with his laptop. 'I was looking for the best route to Beckford's tower. We probably should start there.'

'The notebook. You told me that Miss LeVine took an old leather notebook from the church. Myths and legends or something.'

'No,' said Capel. 'It had slipped my mind. Did they find it when they went over her house?'

'I don't think so. I haven't got a laptop here with the HOLMES VPN on, so I can't check the system.'

'The what what?'

'Virtual private network, to get into the police system and check if your book has been logged as evidence. I wasn't going to Marlborough today, but I will have to nip into the Bath station later: I can check from there. Apart from anything else, you ought to have the notebook back at some point.'

'That's true,' said Capel. 'I'd really like to read it – I've never got round to it.'

There was a knock at the door. Capel pushed back

his chair. 'He's early. I'll go.' As he stood up, his mobile rang. 'Sorry, can you get the door, Vicky?'

'No problem.'

Capel didn't recognise the number. Work calls usually came on the landline. 'Hello, Stephen Capel.'

'Ah, lovely, Reverend Capel. I don't think we've met. My name is Cherie Taylor.'

'The writer?'

'You've heard of me? How sweet.' She pronounced it schweet.

'Er, yes, I assume you know that I've been involved in the murder investigation for Margaret LeVine.'

'Oh, I know. How terrible that must be. The thing is, Margaret told me that you were putting on a little literary festival. This sounds heartless but, I assume Margaret would have been speaking at it… now she's, er, not available, I was wondering if you would want to, erm, take on another historical fiction author? It happens I'm available and I'm quite local. I would love to help out.'

'I'm really sorry,' said Capel. 'After Margaret's death we decided it would be best not to hold the festival this year. It somehow didn't seem appropriate. We might go ahead next year, and I'd certainly get in touch about that when we know more, if you can let me have an email address.'

Vicky had come back into the kitchen with Russell Levine just visible behind her in the hall. 'Who is it?' she mouthed.

Capel put his hand over the bottom of the phone. 'That other author, Cherie Taylor.'

Vicky jumped forward, her hand out. 'Give. We haven't had a chance to speak to her yet.'

'Hang on,' said Capel down the phone. 'I've got someone here who needs to speak to you urgently.' He passed the phone over to Vicky.

'Hello?' Taylor said. 'Who's there?'

'My name is Victoria Denning,' said Vicky. 'I'm a detective constable working on Margaret LeVine's case. We've been trying to contact you, Ms Taylor. We've emailed, left messages on both your phone numbers and called your agent.'

'I'm so sorry,' said Taylor. 'When I've got a book in the early gestation period, as I have now, I like to get a few days away from it all. I go camping, entirely off the grid. Back to nature – it's so refreshing. When you write historical fiction as I do, it can be really important to detach yourself from the modern world and become immersed in the reality of the land. I try not to use anything electrical.'

'Okay. But we need to speak to you as soon as possible. Where are you now?'

'I'm at… hang on, that's the door.'

'Ms Taylor?' Vicky could hear footsteps on the other end of the line, then a door opening.

Muffled, at a distance, Taylor's voice said 'What a surprise! I didn't expect… what do you think? What on earth is…' there was a loud crack and the line went dead.

'Ms Taylor? Are you okay? Ms Taylor?'

'What's happening?' said Capel.

'Phone 999,' said Vicky. 'No, hang on, shit, I don't know where she was. I need to call this in. Something's just happened to Cherie Taylor while she was on the phone to me. It just went dead.' Vicky quickly rang Taylor back, but the call went straight to voicemail.

Vicky flicked through her contacts list to the number for the Marlborough incident room.

'Hello, Sergeant Crawford here.'

'Sarge, we've got a problem. This is Vicky Denning. Cherie Taylor called – you know, the author, person of interest associated with Margaret LeVine – we've been struggling to contact her, but she rang. Only while I was speaking to her, she was cut off. It sounded like someone else was there, possibly an attack. It didn't feel good.'

'Where?' said Crawford.

'She didn't say, but she was inside a building and she answered the door – so it seems likely she was at home.'

'Okay, we'll get a car round there. Hang on.'

Vicky could hear Crawford talking faintly on the other end. She put her hand over the microphone. 'You might as well go without me,' she said to Capel. 'This sounds serious.'

'You still there?' Crawford said.

'Yes.'

'Where are you at the moment?'

'At home. In Thornton Down – near Bath.'

'Okay, Cherie Taylor's home is in Melksham, closer to you than to us. We'll try to get a local car to check the place out, but it would help if you can you head out there now to take charge. We'll be over as quick as we can.'

'Right, okay,' said Vicky, 'I'll do that.'

'Is there someone you can take with you? I'm not comfortable with you going in alone, just in case the local woodentops don't arrive on time.'

'Capel's here,' said Vicky.

'He'll do,' said Crawford. 'One quick question.

How come the Taylor woman had your number?'

'She didn't. She rang Capel. Margaret LeVine must have given her his number, because of this literary festival he was thinking of organising.'

'Right,' said Crawford. 'I'm texting her home address to this phone. Let's hope to God she's actually there. Go. Now.'

Vicky handed the phone back to Capel. 'Change of plan. The sergeant wants me to take you and head to Cherie Taylor's house. Mr Levine, I'm really sorry, but we can't take you with us. This is an emergency.'

'That's okay,' said Levine. 'How about I drive into Bath and meet you at Beckford's tower this afternoon? You've got my number. Just let me know if you aren't going to make it.'

Vicky had been urging them out of the vicarage as Levine spoke. 'Thanks, Mr Levine. We'll see you there.'

Capel locked the door and bundled into Vicky's Golf, waving to Levine. 'Blues and twos?' he said hopefully as Vicky got into the driving seat.

'I really hate TV cop shows,' said Vicky. 'But, yes, you can have some pretty lights. The siren will have to wait until we hit traffic.' She started the concealed flashing lights, revved the car and shot backwards out of the drive, sending gravel flying.

CHAPTER 13

'This is Melksham,' said Vicky. 'Where now?' She flipped the siren on for a few seconds until a white van that was blocking her way had pulled over to the side of the road.

'Turn left at the roundabout into Lowbourne,' said Capel. 'Then across a pair of mini-roundabouts into Forest Road and by the Pig and Whistle across another pair of mini-roundabouts into Woodrow Road. That's where the house is. They do like a good mini-roundabout in Melksham.'

'Okay… Get out of the way!' A cyclist was riding slowly along in the middle of the carriageway. The opposite side of the road was blocked by a queue, leaving no room to overtake. Vicky gave a quick blast of the siren, waited for the cyclist to pull over and shot past.

'Slow down,' said Capel. 'It's one of the houses ahead on the left.' The properties were getting larger and smarter as they got through to the outskirts of the town. Capel glanced down at his phone, where he had pulled up a picture of Taylor's house on Streetview. 'There, that one after the place with the big vegetable garden. The house with the garage extension.'

'Got it,' said Vicky. The gates to an attractive old cottage were open – she swept the Golf round onto the gravel drive, pulling up alongside a battered old Volvo estate. 'She's no J. K. Rowling if her car's anything to go by.'

'Most writers aren't exactly rolling in it,' said Capel. 'Nice house, though.'

Vicky stood by the car, looking back down the road towards the centre of Melksham. 'Our woodentop saviours should have been here by now.'

'Did you like it when they called you a woodentop when you were in uniform?'

'I got called worse. What goes around comes around.'

Capel frowned. 'Do you want to wait?'

Vicky shook her head and pushed her fringe away from her eyes. 'No. Things sounded pretty dire on the phone. Stay behind me.' She picked up a collapsible baton from the car door pocket, flicked it open and strode up to the front door.

Capel followed close behind. 'Is it locked?'

Vicky nodded. 'Looks it.' She pressed the bell push but couldn't hear it ring inside. After a moment she rapped on the door with the handle of the baton. 'Ms Taylor?' She tried the door handle. 'Yep, locked.'

'Shall I go round the back?'

Vicky glanced down the road again. Still no sign of reinforcements. 'I shouldn't let you, but we need someone to stay at the front. Be careful. If you find anything open, don't go in, come straight back and tell me. Actually, better still…' She pulled out her phone and called Capel, waiting for him to answer. 'Okay, keep talking to me as you go round.'

There was a narrow strip of grass between the end of the house's extension and the fence to the next property. Capel hurried along the side of the building. 'I'm nearly at the corner.'

'Take a quick peek round and pull back straight away.'

Capel glanced round the back. 'No one there. A big grass lawn, bit of a patio by the back door. No open windows.'

'Okay, try the door.'

Capel jogged from the corner of the house to the door, about two thirds of the way along the building. It was locked. He glanced through the kitchen window alongside. 'The door's locked. I can't see anyone inside.'

'Right. Get back here. I think we have reasonable cause to break in. The occupant could be in immediate danger.'

Capel hurried back around the building. 'Can I try? I've always wanted to break a door down.'

Vicky sighed. 'Bloody amateurs. Okay, you might as well be the one to get… What are you doing?'

'Getting ready to charge it.'

'You don't use your shoulder, idiot, you'll end up in a lot of pain and a door that's still shut. See where the lock is? Kick as close as you can to that without falling over. At the edge of the door by the lock.'

Capel shrugged. 'Spoilsport.' He took aim and smashed his foot into the door. It shook, but didn't open. 'I felt it move.'

'Another time.'

Capel tried to focus his mind on his foot, brought it up and sent his Doc Marten boot smashing into the varnished wood of the door. There was a satisfying crunch and the door burst open, but stopped when it had moved a few centimetres.

There was just room to get a head through the gap. Vicky peeked in. She breathed in sharply.

'What is it?'

'Help me push the door open enough to get past. Gently. There's someone lying right behind it.'

They pushed on the door until they could squeeze

through. Vicky crouched down alongside the woman who was lying on the floor. She was dressed like a TV wardrobe department's idea of a what an eccentric writer should wear, a kind of aging hippy chic. Vicky felt for a pulse, first on the woman's neck, then her wrist.

'Well?'

Vicky shook her head. 'We're too late. I'll call it in. Can you ring Roland for me? I'd like him out here ASAP if we can get him. The locals have not inspired me with confidence so far.'

Capel fought back the urge to make the usual sarcastic comment about Vicky's godfather and found McLean in his contacts list.

While Capel was waiting for an answer, Vicky started speaking on her phone. 'Me again, Sarge. I'm afraid she's dead. No, they haven't…'

'Hello?' Capel frowned. It was a female voice, a voice that was somehow familiar, but that he couldn't pin down out of context.

'Sorry,' said Capel, 'is that Roland Mclean's number? I need to speak to him urgently.'

'Yes, of course. Roland!'

'Mclean.'

'Roland, it's Capel. I'm with Vicky in Melksham. We're at the house of Cherie Taylor, a person of interest in the Margaret LeVine case. She appears to be dead, but we spoke to her on the phone only about half an hour ago, so it's very recent. Can you come and have a look, now? Vicky would really appreciate your opinion.'

'Sounds fun,' said Mclean. 'Text me the address. I'll get there as quickly as I can.'

Capel hung up and sent the details to Mclean.

'I will,' Vicky said down her phone. 'That's good, thanks. Hang on a moment.' She put her hand over the mouthpiece and grimaced at Capel. 'Did you get through to Roland?'

'He's on his way.'

'Okay, thanks.' Vicky put the phone back to her ear. 'I've asked Dr Mclean to come over… I know SOCO will, but I can't see any obvious cause of death. I thought it would be a good idea if Dr Mclean could see her as soon as possible in situ given the unusual circumstances… Yes, I will. Bye.'

'Were they not impressed with your initiative?'

'A bit twitchy. SOCO can get territorial about these things, but they agreed it was a good idea.'

'So, what now?'

'A quick look round while we wait.' Vicky handed Capel a pair of disposable gloves. 'Don't wander round more than you have to. Don't touch things for the sake of it. Just mentally flag anything that needs attention.'

'How about her phone?' asked Capel. He pointed to the mobile, on the floor about a metre from the body.

'That definitely needs attention.' Vicky picked it up and pressed the button on the side. 'Dead,' she said.

'Must have been damaged when she dropped it,' said Capel.

'Maybe, though the screen's still in one piece.'

There was a burst of siren outside, followed by the crunch of gravel, heard through the open front door. Vicky sighed. 'Here comes the cavalry.'

CHAPTER 14

'Vic!'

Vicky looked up at Capel and smiled. They were both in Taylor's office, just off the hallway. Mclean's voice from the outside sounded intensely pleased with himself.

Capel opened the door to see the pathologist in full protective gear standing over the body, shooing a uniformed officer out of the way. 'Hello, Roland.'

'Capel. You do like to fill my days for me, don't you?'

Vicky squeezed into the doorway alongside Capel. 'Don't blame him, this one's down to me.'

'If you're confessing all, that'll save me a job,' said Mclean. 'How far have SOCO got?'

'They're not here yet,' said Vicky. 'So, it's minimal interaction. But I just hoped you could give us some idea of what happened to her. I can't see any marks on the body. She was talking to me on the phone. Someone came to the door, then seconds later she dropped the phone. Whatever it was, it was quick.'

'We can't rule out a coincidental heart attack,' said Mclean. 'I know no one likes a coincidence, but realistically they do happen all the time in the grand scheme of things. You know, when I was at university, I once ran into someone I knew from Oxford, crossing a zebra crossing in a village two hundred miles away. The chances against someone winning the lottery are something like 45 million to one against – but people do still win. Hmm. Her appearance is entirely consistent with having suffered a cardiac arrest.' He pulled up the face mask that was beneath his chin, bent over the body, and pulled back the top of Taylor's loose dress, making her extravagant bead necklaces rattle. 'Aha.'

'Aha?' said Vicky.

'I need a moment.' Mclean took out his phone and pulled up Google.

Capel squeezed past Mclean and into the kitchen. 'There's something odd in here,' he called out to Vicky.

'It's definitely an aha,' said Mclean.

'Don't make me use force on you,' said Vicky.

'She has a pacemaker,' said Mclean. 'I think we may have the cause of death, at least the direct cause.'

'Her pacemaker failed?'

'That's unlikely,' said Mclean. 'Modern pacemakers are very efficient and well-monitored to anticipate failure to enable them to be dealt with before it happens.'

'So, what are you saying? That her visitor did something to it?'

'Can you come in here a moment, please?' said Capel.

'Spoil my moment, won't you,' grumbled Mclean, but he eased himself up from the kneeling position and followed Vicky into the kitchen.

'What's not right here?' said Capel, waving at the kitchen fittings.

'Well…' Vicky looked around her. 'The clock's stopped. Pretty much exactly the same time as we got the call. Another coincidence?'

'Mm-hm,' said Capel. He picked up the landline phone, holding the handset near his ear without it touching him. 'No sound. It's dead. And the clock on the cooker is dead too. Same time. And that fancy electronic hob isn't working. Neither is the microwave. And her laptop. And her phone. Every bit of electronics in this place is dead.'

Mclean sucked his lip. 'That would seem to confirm the diagnosis you prevented me from giving. Have you heard of an EMP device?'

Capel frowned. 'It sounds familiar.'

'Electromagnetic pulse device,' said Mclean. 'It's a specialist hi-tech weapon.'

'The Matrix,' said Vicky. 'The flying submarine thingy uses one in The Matrix against the nasty mechanical squid thing.'

'Very lucid. Still hoping for a job reviewing films, are we?' asked Mclean.

'I get it,' said Capel. 'But aren't EMPs just science fiction?'

Mclean shook his head. 'They certainly exist, though I think the major military ones are small nuclear devices that are exploded in the air and wipe out anything electronic across a few miles radius. I am not familiar with anything more focused.'

'I know a man who would be,' said Capel.

By now a SOCO van had arrived, along with reinforcements from Marlborough and they were all ushered out into the garden. Capel was looking up EMPs on his phone when Vicky tapped him on the shoulder.

'The guv says to get out from under foot,' Vicky said. 'We'll have to give statements later but there's not a lot we can do for the moment.'

'Okay,' said Capel, following her to the car. 'Do you mind if I give Ed a ring? If anyone knows about secret government technology…'

'Be my guest,' said Vicky.

Vicky was heading back for the centre of Melksham when Capel got through. 'Hi, Ed – could you spare a minute?'

'Anything for you,' replied Ed. 'As long as no money is going to change hands. From my end, I mean: you are welcome to pay for the service.'

'Is there such a thing as a small, portable EMP device?'

'No, of course not.' said Ed. 'They are technically infeasible. All official indications are that they do not, and cannot, exist.'

'How about unofficial indications?'

'The answer is still no. That's what we call plausible deniability. But let's say it wouldn't surprise me if certain elements of the security services had access to devices with an effect that was remarkably similar to what you might expect an EMP to do. This is purely hypothetical, you realise.'

'And could you find out if such a hypothetical device has hypothetically gone missing?'

'I'll have a word with a few non-existent people and get back to you about what I don't know.'

Vicky swore under her breath as a car pulled out right in front of her. 'Any help from Ed?'

'He's going to get back to me about what he doesn't know.' Capel saw Vicky's response on her face. 'Don't ask.' He checked his phone. 'I think maybe we should have an early lunch, then we can meet up with Russell Levine about two o'clock. There'd still be time then to pop over to Margaret's house after, if you can get the key. It would be good to see if that missing notebook was there.'

'Sounds like a plan,' said Vicky.

~

Capel had decided the taxi needed an outing. Vicky was never hugely enthusiastic about using it, but it was a bright afternoon of late autumn sunlight, and it somehow seemed to detach them a little from the scene at Cherie Taylor's house, so she had agreed.

'There, on the left,' Vicky said as they headed up Lansdown Road out of the centre of Bath, passing a new looking housing development on the right. 'Stop in the layby there.'

'Are you sure?' asked Capel. I can't see this tower and it looks like we're heading well out of town here. Have we come too far?'

'Just pull in.'

Capel drew the taxi up behind a short line of cars in the layby. There was no pavement. On the other side of the stone wall they had parked beside were grave markers. 'This is definitely it,' said Vicky. She led the way along the grass verge that started after the layby.

'Oh, good grief,' said Capel. He stopped abruptly, taking hold of the ornate iron railing that topped the section of wall beside them to stabilise himself. 'The bishop.'

'Where?' said Vicky, peering through the railing. 'There's no one there.'

'No, not here,' said Capel. 'When I rang Roland.'

'You have totally lost me. And quite possibly totally lost the plot too.'

'When I rang Roland from Cherie Taylor's house, a woman answered. I was sure I knew the voice, but I couldn't place it. I've just realised, it was Bishop

Emma. My bishop. She was at Roland's.'

'Are you sure?'

'Absolutely certain. They met the other year, didn't they? You don't think…'

'He did say he had a new lady friend last time we had a chat. We'll have to keep an eye on them at the wedding.'

Capel nodded. 'Oh, rather grand.' He pointed ahead to the Romanesque archway that pierced the next section of stone wall, which was much higher. A pair of padlocked wrought iron gates blocked the main drive, but at the left-hand side was a narrow open gateway. A rather antiquated looking sign proclaimed this was the entrance to both Lansdown Burial Ground and Beckford's Tower and Museum. 'After you,' Capel said.

Vicky walked through the dank entranceway into the chilly sunlight beyond. To their right, a high, square tower, topped with an ornate cupola, loomed over the graveyard. The path led to the two-storey building at the base of the tower. Levine was standing near the doorway, waiting for them.

'Thanks for this,' said Levine as they approached.

'It's no trouble,' said Capel. 'To be honest, I'm embarrassed I've lived near Bath a few years now and I've never visited here before.'

The main part of the ground floor of the building was closed off, with a discreet sign saying that it could be booked as accommodation through the Landmark Trust, but the elegant spiral staircase that continued all the way up the tower led them to the first floor, which now housed the museum. An elderly lady on the door to the museum had the appearance of eccentricity that seemed to be a requirement to work at such a venue. She was dressed in black from head to foot, with a hat that seemed to be made of crow feathers. Her eyes were a piercing icy blue. The only touch of colour on her dress was a badge with a tasteful grey-on-white rendering of the tower and 'Miss Rickman' in a sans serif, heritage-friendly font.

'Welcome to Beckford's Tower. It's ten pounds per person, but you do get a pamphlet.'

Capel muttered 'That's alright, then,' ending in a splutter as Vicky elbowed him in the stomach.

'This is on me,' said Levine. 'You are doing me a favour by coming.' He produced a fifty-pound note.

Miss Rickman looked at the note with suspicion. 'Do you have anything else? We don't like fifty-pound notes.'

'I'm sorry,' said Levine. 'Do you take cards?'

Miss Rickman looked at him as if he had brought in dog muck on his shoes. 'Certainly not. We like those even less. I suppose you appear respectable.'

'I am a vicar,' said Capel.

'Hmm,' said Miss Rickman, looking at Capel's open-necked shirt with a similar degree of distrust to that she had applied the note. 'It's not obvious.'

'It's my day off,' said Capel.

'He really is a vicar,' said Vicky, producing her warrant card. 'And I am a police officer. I would be very grateful if you could take Mr Levine's payment. I can vouch for him.'

'Very well,' said Miss Rickman. 'Just make sure that they don't touch anything.'

'I certainly will,' said Vicky, nodding at Capel. 'I frequently have to with this one.'

Capel took the guide leaflets Miss Rickman was proffering as Levine picked up his change.

'Proceed around in a clockwise fashion, following the arrows,' said Miss Rickman. 'Feel free to return to me if you have any questions.'

They passed through into the next room, which was kitted out like a cross between a museum and a stately home. 'I'm sorry,' said Capel to Vicky, 'what exactly does "I frequently have to" mean?'

'Sorry,' said Vicky, 'I was just trying to ingratiate myself with her.'

'Hmm,' said Capel.

'So, what exactly are we looking for?' asked Levine.

'Ignore us,' said Capel. 'As I mentioned, Margaret said that there was an Anglo-Saxon brooch found when they dug the Combe Down tunnel. I don't suppose the brooch can tell us much in itself about Alfred, but she thought there was accompanying documentation from when it was found, and that could give us some context. For that matter, the brooch does give an idea of just how rich this Bath reeve was.'

They strolled around, checking the cases where something the size of a brooch might be on display. The collection was, to say the least, eclectic – a mix of items collected on William Beckford's travels and items of trendy interior décor from the 1800s.

'Did you know that this place was briefly a pub?' asked Capel, glancing through the pamphlet. 'And then a chapel for the cemetery. I always feel there's a strong natural connection between the clergy and beer. Of course, monks used to brew it.'

Levine, who had got ahead of them, headed back over, shaking his head. 'Nothing. It's mostly fancy furniture and the odd painting, but there's nothing resembling an Anglo-Saxon brooch. I think we're going to have to face the crow woman again.'

'I'll have a go,' said Capel. 'Old ladies usually get on well with vicars.'

'What are you saying?' asked Vicky.

Capel shook his head and strode through to where Miss Rickman sat. 'Hello, it's us again.'

'Isn't it just?' said Miss Rickman. 'Are you heading up to the belvedere?'

'Definitely,' said Capel. 'But we wanted to check something with you first, as you obviously know a lot about this place. We were told that Beckford's collection included an Anglo-Saxon brooch found near Combe Down, but we couldn't see it.'

'That would be because most of William Beckford's collection isn't here anymore,' said Miss Rickman. 'When he died in 1844, his collection was mostly sold off. Some of it went abroad, but you will also find substantial portions in the Victoria and Albert Museum in London, the British Museum, the Wallace Collection, The National Gallery and at locations throughout the country. This brooch could be at any one of these. For that matter, a significant amount of what's generally described as his collection was in reality added after his death, and was never in this building. I have a small volume on Beckford's treasures and their current locations, which you may purchase for a nominal sum.'

'I'll get this one,' said Vicky. She paid Miss Rickman and took the booklet, flicking through the pages. 'I see what you mean, there are bits of the collection all over the place. Some went abroad.'

'There,' said Capel, peering over Vicky's shoulder. He pointed to an illustration of a triptych painting.

'That's not a brooch,' said Vicky.

'Read the words,' said Capel.

'Okay. "The Fitzwilliam collection includes the 1538 triptych The Lamentation with the Prophet Daniel and St Peter by Pierre Reymond and an exquisite Anglo-Saxon brooch, both typifying Beckford's taste, although the brooch was the last item added to the collection, long after his death.'

'So the brooch is not exactly local, then,' said Levine.

'No, in Cambridge,' said Vicky.

'I'm not doing anything tomorrow,' said Capel. 'Vicky and I could take a look. We've been talking about visiting Cambridge for ages.'

'If you're sure,' said Levine. 'Perhaps you could let me know what you find out.'

'Of course,' said Capel.

'We've still got the tunnel to see,' said Vicky. 'And we should try the belvedere before we go. What is a belvedere?'

'I'm glad you asked,' said Miss Rickman. Vicky jumped – the old woman had been sitting quietly, listening to their discussion with interest. 'A belvedere is a structure specifically designed to give a good view out over the surroundings. From the Italian, bel vedere, to view beauty. That's what we have here.'

'What are we waiting for?' said Capel. 'Thank you, Miss Rickman.'

Miss Rickman smiled faintly, then pointedly picked up a magnifying glass and began carefully examining Levine's fifty-pound note.

The view was, indeed, attractive, both back down to the city and looking out across the greener vistas to the west. 'You can't see Combe Down from here,' said Capel, but we'll be heading in that general direction.' He pointed out of the opening in the octagonal structure.

They walked back to the stairway. 'After you,' said Capel.

'No, after you,' said Levine.

'She won't bite,' said Vicky. 'I'll go first.'

CHAPTER 15

'I don't remember it looking like this,' said Capel.

'It's a while since we came before,' said Vicky. They had driven in convoy from the tower and parked at the side of the lane that wound its way through Thornton Down out westward into the countryside. The map on her phone put the nearest point to park beside a footpath sign at the side of the lane. From there, the path led a few hundred metres to the tunnel itself.

Capel pointed to a sign near the entrance. 'It's 1670 metres, it seems. Lighting in operation 05.00 to 23.00 – and just in case you don't understand these fancy time formats, they kindly have another notice to tell us this means they're switched off from 11pm to 5am. I have no intention of still being here then.'

'I think we did it last time in less than the predicted 25 minutes, though,' said Vicky. 'Surely that's less than 3 miles per hour.'

As they walked in through the entrance, they were surrounded by a gentle swirl of ambient string music. Ahead, the lights on either side of the tunnel led forward to converge in the distance. The path seemed straight, but its gradual descent meant they could not see the far entrance yet.

'It's longer than I expected,' said Levine.

'Yes,' said Capel. 'To be honest, even if there's some kind of marker where the brooch was found, there's little chance of spotting it without a way to pin down the location.' He ran his hand along the tunnel wall. It felt slightly damp. Most of it seemed to be a greyish brick, but on some stretches it looked more like the tunnel had been hewed out of solid rock.

'What was that?' said Vicky. They all stopped, listening, hearing a strange mix of squeaks and creaks, just audible above the recorded music. Far ahead, a dark shadow lurched in the middle of the tunnel.

'Peter Finch did hint that there might be a ghost train,' said Capel. 'Apparently, in the 1920s a steam train crew was asphyxiated here. It was an unusually long tunnel not to have any ventilation. The train just ran on with a dead man at the controls.'

'Don't be melodramatic,' said Vicky, 'it's a bike.'

They could now make out the shape more clearly as the moving shape occluded the blue-white lights lining the tunnel. The bike was hurtling towards them down the middle of the tunnel. They hesitated, not sure which side to go for, then Capel and Levine followed Vicky over to the left-hand side, standing on a narrow, pebbled verge against the wall.

The cyclist shot past, a gloved hand raised and shouted 'Thanks!' back to them.

'Not that we had a lot of choice,' said Levine.

By now, the end of the tunnel, a small blob of light, had lifted up from the floor ahead. It grew larger faster than Vicky expected, until they were looking out of a rectangular gated entrance, the top of the tunnel's curvature cut off by panelling. They came out of the tunnel into a green cutting, framed by the leafless trees.

'That was interesting,' said Levine. 'Though not something I would want to do every day. I think I'm going to head on for a bit. I've got the day off and I enjoy a good walk.'

'We probably need to get back,' said Vicky.

'There's another, shorter tunnel ahead if you go on for a bit.'

'Thanks,' said Levine. 'So, you two are going to Cambridge tomorrow?'

'That's the plan,' said Capel. 'Nice to meet you again.'

They shook hands, and Capel and Vicky turned back to the tunnel.

'Are you feeling okay?' Capel asked. 'I mean, we did find a body only a few hours ago.'

'Don't go all caring vicar on me. I know death is part of your work, but you're not usually in the business of discovering murder victims either. How are you feeling?'

'Touché,' said Capel. 'All I could really say is that I feel a bit numb. It doesn't seem real.'

'That's it,' said Vicky. 'I know we're supposed to talk everything out endlessly, but to be honest, until we know more all I want to do is to push it to the back of mind and get on with things.'

~

After just over three hours' drive on Saturday morning, Vicky pulled into the Trumpington Park and Ride. 'This place sounds like something from an old children's TV show,' she said.

'That was Trumpton,' said Capel. 'This is Trumpington. But I get the point.'

'It's close enough. But are you sure it's sensible parking here? We're still about three miles from Cambridge.'

'Driving into the centre's a nightmare, and the road network is deliberately set up to make it difficult for drivers. The bus takes us right to the Fitzwilliam museum. There's a stop outside.'

The park and ride bus was waiting when they got to the stop. They hurried to get onboard and out of the biting wind. As soon as they had settled into their seats at the front of the upper deck, the bus pulled out and headed down the road towards the city. 'I like buses,' said Capel. 'I don't know why we don't use them more.'

'Because there isn't a bus to Thornton Down?' said Vicky.

'Fair point.'

They passed through the village and into the outskirts of the city. 'The Botanic Gardens are over there,' said Capel, pointing to the right. 'One of the many interesting sites I never saw while I was at university. When you live somewhere, you don't see it properly.'

A large, white classical structure loomed up ahead on the left. 'That's it,' said Capel, 'the Fitzwilliam.'

The bus pulled up right in front of the high portico. 'That is impressive,' said Vicky.

'I actually have been here,' said Capel, 'but I can't remember much about it.'

They climbed the steps at the front and into the entrance hall. An information desk was positioned centrally between two flights of stairs. Capel approached and spoke to a smiling young man with thick glasses and dreadlocks. 'Do you know where we'll find Anglo-Saxon exhibits?'

'We don't have an Anglo-Saxon gallery as such, but I know we have a good number of Anglo-Saxon coins, and some artefacts, particularly from the King's Field dig in Faversham. If you go across to Gallery 32

– it's hiding at the back of the armoury gallery, up that way, over to the left and then right. Ask the attendant there.'

'Thanks,' said Vicky.

The gallery held a mix of medieval and renaissance pieces, mostly more recent than they were looking for. The attendant was also young, a woman this time. 'Hi,' said Capel, 'we're looking for an Anglo-Saxon artefact. It's a brooch, originally from near Bath.'

'Just a moment,' said the woman. She picked up a tablet from beside her chair and did a quick search. 'Oh, yes, over here.' She led the way across the narrow gallery. 'Most of the Anglo-Saxon exhibits came to us in a single bequest in the early 1900s, but this was donated earlier, I think.' She pointed at a small display case containing only a carefully-lit brooch. It was a curved disk of gold, nearly as wide as a fist, with an orange star in the centre, patterned around with inlays of red enamel.

'It's beautiful,' said Vicky. 'You could wear that today.'

'You could,' said the attendant. 'Though I think the insurance would be quite high.'

'Is there any accompanying documentation?' asked Vicky. She produced her warrant card. 'We are looking for information in connection with a police investigation.'

The attendant looked worried. 'According to the record, this brooch was acquired in the nineteenth century. There has never been any suggestion that it was stolen. It would have been logged here.'

'No,' said Vicky, 'that's not what it's about. This has nothing to do with theft, it is just important for us to discover any information there is about the discovery of the brooch in connection to a totally separate investigation. Do you have any documentation from its donation?'

The attendant looked back at the tablet and started to flick through options. 'Hang on, it came to us rather indirectly… Yes, there's something… Oh, I see.'

Capel smiled encouragingly after a few seconds of silence.

'Sorry,' said the attendant. 'There is a document covering the brooch's discovery, but we don't have it here at the museum. It's in the university library. You need to speak to… erm, just a minute. A Doctor Schmidt. I'll get you the phone number to make an appointment.'

~

'Now that's what I call a library,' said Vicky. 'I suppose you spent ages here when you were doing your degree.'

'Strangely, no,' said Capel. 'I came here twice in three years, for reasons I now forget. Something related to music, I think. There really wasn't a lot of need to come here doing a maths course.' He followed Vicky through to the front desk. 'We're here to see Doctor Schmidt.'

'One moment.' The librarian tapped on a screen. 'She's expecting you. Down the corridor there, up one flight of stairs and it's the second room on the right. Name's on the door.'

'Thanks,' said Vicky.

Doctor Schmidt's office door was propped open with a mountainous pile of books. She stood to greet them as Vicky led the way in. 'Good morning.'

'It's very good of you to see us,' said Capel, 'especially on a Saturday.'

'I'm lucky in my job,' said Schmidt. Her German accent was only just noticeable. 'I can choose which days to work. I'd much rather work at the weekend, then I can take days off when things are quieter. If you can ever call a day quiet during term time in Cambridge.'

'I'm Detective Constable Denning,' said Vicky, showing her warrant card. 'This is Reverend Capel.'

'Just Capel,' said Capel. 'I tend to work at the weekend and have time off during the week as well, though that's more a function of the job description.'

Schmidt smiled. 'I gather this is about the Beckford brooch documentation. I had it sent up from the stacks to save time.' She sorted through a pile of cardboard files on her desk and pulled out one containing a single sheet of paper. 'Have you seen the brooch?'

'Yes,' said Capel, 'we've come straight from the Fitzwilliam. It's a remarkable thing.'

'Hmm,' said Schmidt. She peered at the document. 'So, this document was provided to the museum along with the bill of sale. They should still have that at the museum if you need to see it. This document appears to describe the finding of the brooch when a railway tunnel was being dug: quite interesting. Here, please look.'

'Do you mind if I take it out of the folder to photograph it?' asked Vicky.

'Go ahead,' said Schmidt. 'The paper is not sensitive, nor is this what we would consider a historically significant document. No need for gloves.'

Vicky pulled the single sheet out of the folder. 'It's

not A4, is it?' She took a couple of shots of the document with her phone.

Schmidt smiled. 'No, it's foolscap. This was a common paper size in the UK until the 1960s, when the European A sizes were introduced. It's an amusing name.'

'Was it the right shape to make a dunce's cap?' asked Capel.

'No. This size of paper traditionally had a watermark with a jester's head on, wearing a fool's cap. The floppy kind with bells, not the pointy dunce cap you are thinking of. There are rumours that the watermark was first used by the sixteenth century paper mill owner Sir John Spielmann, whose surname is the German for jester, but there's no evidence for this. And it's sometimes supposed to have been used as a dig by the Rump Parliament, aimed at the executed King Charles the First, because they replaced the royal coat of arms on the watermark by this fool. But that also is a myth, I'm sad to say. It's just a watermark.'

Capel picked the sheet of paper up and read it aloud. 'Here we go: "A remarkable find fortuitously resultant from the construction of the Combe Down Tunnel. During the digging of the tunnel for the Somerset and Dorset Railway in 1873, this brooch was uncovered by inland navigators. One, an itinerant Irish labourer named Joseph Donnelly, seems to have been the first to find the item, but was attacked by fellow-workers, as happens all too frequently in alcohol-fuelled disputes amongst these common labourers.

"Donnelly was fatally injured, and for some weeks after the attack the brooch disappeared, but it was later pawned in Bath, where it was brought to the attention of the authorities. The brooch was recovered and bought by the Scottish nobleman William Alexander Douglas-Hamilton, the twelfth Duke Hamilton, who had inherited William Beckford's collection via Beckford's daughter Susanna, Douglas-Hamilton's grandmother. The Douglas-Hamilton collection was dispersed in the Hamilton Palace sale of 1882, when the brooch was purchased by the Fitzwilliam Museum." So we were on something of a wild goose chase in Bath. The brooch was never kept at Beckford's Tower, it has just become associated with the Beckford collection.'

'What else does it say?' asked Vicky.

'It's mostly just a description. "Fine Anglo-Saxon disc brooch in enamelled gold, decorated with an ornate pattern featuring a central star and elegant repeated forms." Blah, blah. "Although the disc brooch was far more common between the fifth and seventh centuries, from the decorative design this example appears to be of later design, perhaps as late as the ninth century." More technical stuff. Ah, yes. "Although there was speculation that the find could have been part of a larger buried hoard, the exigencies" – excellent word, exigencies, you don't see it often enough – "the exigencies of tunnel construction meant that the site of the find was rapidly covered by the tunnel walls, meaning that nothing further is known to have been found." Blah, blah, signed Basil Christie and dated 15 March 1885. So, if there were other artefacts, they should still be there.'

'Is that what this is about?' asked Schmidt. 'A treasure hunt?'

'Not really,' said Vicky. 'It is a murder investigation, I'm afraid. The victim was writing about this period in the locale where the brooch was found and there is some concern that her death may have been associated with the attempt to take over a discovery that the victim made. Has anyone else requested access to this document in the last three months or so?'

Schmidt turned to her computer, made a few mouse clicks and shook her head. 'Looking at the log, as far as I can tell no one has ever viewed this document since it came into the possession of the library. To be honest, digitisation of the early logs has not been completed, but we can certainly say there has been no access requested in the last twenty years, though, yes, there was a query relatively recently.' She peered at her computer screen. 'A Margaret LeVine made an enquiry about the existence of the document, but she never took it further.'

'What date was that?' asked Vicky.

'The fourth of October this year.'

'Just over a week before Margaret died,' said Capel.

'This Margaret LeVine was your victim?' asked Schmidt. 'I don't know how I feel about that.'

'Yes, I'm afraid it was her,' said Vicky. She peered over Capel's shoulder at the document. 'What's that at the bottom of the page?'

'It could be decorative,' said Capel. 'Some squiggles, that's all. Almost looks is if someone has used this as a bit of scrap paper to keep a tally.'

'May I?' said Schmidt. She took the sheet of paper from Capel, turned on her desk light and brought the bottom of the document up to within a few centimetres of her eyes. 'I really must get new reading glasses. It would be very unusual for a document like this to be decorated just for the fun of it. We're not talking about an illuminated medieval manuscript. My suspicion is that this is meant to convey something, but I'm not at all sure what. As you say, it could just be casual use of the document as scrap paper. It happens more than you would think, even with the most precious manuscripts.'

'Let me get a close up of that bit,' said Vicky, pulling her phone out again. 'Got it.' She pushed the document back across the desk to Schmidt. 'Thank you very much for your help.'

'It's been a pleasure,' said Schmidt. 'One of the reasons I love my job is the variety of people I meet, and the different uses they make of library resources.'

'I know it's a long shot,' said Vicky, passing her card across, 'but if you find out anything more about this document, or the brooch, could you let me know. There's an email and phone number on the card. At the moment, any scrap of information could be useful. And also, if you can contact me if anyone else requests access.'

'Of course,' said Schmidt.

As Capel and Vicky emerged from the building, a few spots of rain began to fall. 'It's a shame we can't stay over,' said Vicky. 'You've always promised me the proper Cambridge tour. I haven't even seen your college.'

'It's not one of the big tourist numbers,' said Capel. 'Yes, I'd like to show you. But I couldn't stay tonight. I've got an 8.30 Communion in the morning.'

'How far's the college?' asked Vicky.

'Close,' said Capel. 'Less than ten minutes walk.'

'So?'

Capel shrugged. 'It's not very nice weather, and the bus stop is in the opposite direction.'

'I thought you northerners were supposed to be all hardy and weatherproof?'

'I've spent too long with soft southerners. But you're right, this is hardly the worst. This way, madam.'

Capel led the way past the car park at the opposite side of the building to the way they had come in and out onto Grange Road.

'What do you make of those markings on the document?' asked Vicky.

'It could be some sort of code,' said Capel. 'I ought to show it to Ed, it's more his kind of thing.'

'Do that,' said Vicky. 'I'll send you the pictures.' The drizzle started to get heavier: Vicky pulled up her coat collar and shivered.

'That's the university Rugby Ground on the right,' said Capel, pointing to the other side of the road. 'In the second year I had a room with a brilliant view over it.'

'But you hate rugby.'

'Hate is a strong word. I don't hate it; I just have no interest in it. But other people get very excited about the game. I have to confess I hired out my room a couple of times for big matches.'

'You didn't?'

'Not for much. I wasn't that money grubbing. But it was mutual benefit. I didn't go looking to hire it out – they came and asked me.'

They crossed a road, getting a clearer view of a brick and concrete building on the right. 'So that's where your room was?'

Capel nodded. 'Cripps Court. There's a couple of

those in Cambridge. Contributed by someone who made their money from window frames, or something. I definitely remember something about window frames. I was on the second floor of I staircase in the second year and on the ground floor of the same staircase in my last year.'

'What about the first year?'

Capel pointed to the left, past a more modern pair of buildings to a Victorian-looking red brick tower. 'In Old Court, A staircase. Funny the things you remember. In my first year we had bedders called Rose and Belle. Everyone was terrified of them.'

'I'm sorry? Bedders? What is this, some kind of Victorian public school slang for ladies of the night?'

'Hah. And yes, I know before you say it, privilege, blah, blah. Bedders is short for bedmakers. They basically came in and did a quick clean of your rooms. And, well, made the bed.'

Vicky snorted. 'Did they warm your slippers for you? Toast you a crumpet?'

'Hardly. And their bedmaking skills made hospital corners look sloppy. As an experiment one night, I tried sleeping in my bed without loosening the bedclothes. I stayed in the same position all night – it was so tight that it was impossible to even turn over.'

'Oh, it's beautiful,' Vicky said as the frontage of the older part of the college came into view.

'I'm rather fond of it. It's not flash like Kings or Trinity, but it has a certain Victorian charm.' Capel led Vicky through the archway into the square grass court. 'The chapel's across there, as you can see. That's where I picked up my fondness for Tudorbethan church music. On the right up the stairs is the hall. Which was, I admit, a bit of a Hogwarts experience. Whoah!' He grabbed Vicky's arm to stop her walking onto the grass. 'Sorry, habit. On the whole, unless you are a Fellow, walking on the grass is frowned upon.'

'Sorry. Did you miss living in this quadrangle and moving across the road to the modern block?'

'Court,' said Capel. 'Not quadrangle – that's Oxford. Not at all. The room was pretty basic here and we had shared toilets and bathrooms. Cripps Court was more comfortable and had en-suites.'

'And you used to eat in that hall? Really like Hogwarts?'

'Sometimes. In my day there was a formal hall every day but Saturday, and I used to have dinner there most days we sang evensong, which was typically four times a week. The other nights I either had something in my room or went out with friends, or there was a more café-like sitting earlier. And it was only special occasions that it was really Hogwarty. Though we did always wear gowns for formal hall. They used to say it was to stop the waiters spilling soup down your clothes.'

'You're kidding me, right? How long ago were you here, in the middle ages?'

'No, it really was like that. There was even a Latin grace before the meal. Some poor student was roped in each time to say it. I was so grateful it was never me. Though we did once do a jazz amen from the gallery.'

'Sorry?'

'Student prank. The choir hid in the gallery, then at the end of the grace, we popped up and sang a four-part amen before leaving rapidly.'

'Wizard prank, what?'

'Yes, alright. There was a tradition here of quite elegant practical jokes. But as I was saying about the grace, I never said it, and yet I heard it so often, I can still remember it, word for word.'

'You are joking again, right?'

Capel shook his head. 'Ahem. Benedic Domine, nobis et donis Tuis, quae de Tua largitate, erm, oh yes, sumus sumpturi; et concede ut iis muneribus Tuis ad laudem Tuam utamur gratisque animis fruamur, per Jesum Christum Dominum Nostrum. Amen.'

'Wow.'

'Wow indeed. This was read from a lectern alongside the high table. That was a big table on a dais at the top of the hall, where the Fellows sat. As an alumnus I can dine at High Table once a term, though I can only take a guest on special alumni nights, I think.'

'We're going,' said Vicky. 'The next opportunity.'

'Really? I've never done it – it doesn't appeal to me.'

'Yeah, well, some of us haven't had a chance to experience this privileged shit.'

Capel sighed. 'I know it was wonderful to come here – but I think it'd be unfair to call me privileged, in the sense that I didn't go to a public school or come from a posh background. It's mostly millworkers in my family tree. But yes, I'll look into it. I think we'd better get going now. If we do come some other time, I'll give you a proper tour.' He paused as they walked back into the archway under the tower. 'Actually, could you indulge me in one more thing?'

Vicky smiled. 'Go for it.'

'I just want to pop into the Porter's Lodge and buy

a bottle of college port. It's not brilliant, frankly, but it's a bit of a nostalgia thing.'

'Of course it would be,' said Vicky. 'And you must.'

~

On Monday morning, Suki Dawson answered the door in her pyjamas. 'Yes?'

'I'm sorry, Ms Dawson. If you remember, we spoke a few days ago. I'm DC Denning, and this is DC Sutton.'

'No vicar this time?'

'No,' said Vicky, 'not this time. Can we come in? This won't take long. We've been calling you since Thursday evening and haven't managed to catch you.'

'I'm sorry. For once I got to go away with my husband on one of his interminable business trips. I sometimes suspect he would forget his own address if he hadn't got it written down. I like to leave my phone off and get away from it all when I get a chance to go along. I didn't realise you'd called.'

'Is your husband here?' asked Sutton.

'No, he had to go straight on to Leeds – we were in Harrogate before that. Surprisingly nice for the north.'

'We just need to clarify a couple of points,' said Vicky. They followed Dawson into the sitting room. Vicky perched on the sofa opposite her, Sutton stood in the corner with his notebook. 'Have you got a list of committee members of the festival?' Vicky asked.

'Yes. Why?'

'It's just routine. We may need to contact them about Margaret's involvement.'

'Fine. Just a minute.' Dawson went out into the hall and returned a minute later with a sheet of paper. 'Is that all? I have a busy day.'

'Not quite,' said Vicky. 'When I spoke to you previously, you mentioned being here all evening alone on the night of the incident and having an Indian takeaway delivered. We've spoken to the people at the Raj. It appears that it wasn't you who answered the door.'

Dawson smiled tightly. 'I think you will find that I did not say that I was alone, I said that my husband wasn't here, which was the case.'

'So, who was with you?' asked Vicky.

'Is that really important?'

'This is a murder investigation, so yes, it is important.'

'It was Russell, okay? Russell Levine, Margaret's nephew. He's an old friend. We keep each other company sometimes.' She stared straight at Vicky, as if to challenge her to question the exact meaning of her words.

'That's very interesting,' said Sutton. 'When we spoke to Mr Levine about what he was doing on the night of the murder he didn't mention this.'

Dawson shrugged. 'He was hardly going to boast about it, was he? He was just trying to protect me – it really has nothing to do with what happened. I presume Paul, my husband, doesn't need to know? Meeting up with Russell was all above board, of course, but Paul's the jealous kind.'

'We don't discuss aspects of the case with the public where it's not necessary,' said Vicky.

'Is that all you wanted to ask?' said Dawson. 'I need to get dressed – like I said, I've got a full day ahead. I haven't even had breakfast yet.'

'Not exactly,' said Sutton. 'So just to be clear, you are telling us that Mr Levine was lying when he said he was in Hungerford until eight o'clock?'

Dawson frowned. 'Well, yes, I suppose you could call it a lie. But he was only trying to protect my name. As I say, he was here.'

'We'll check on this with Mr Levine,' said Vicky. 'But given the Raj's delivery driver only saw Mr Levine, could you confirm that you were at home all evening? You didn't go out at all?'

'Absolutely,' said Dawson. 'The Mop makes the town centre a nightmare.'

'The thing is,' said Vicky, 'we have CCTV placing you on the High Street on the night in question five minutes before the incident. You were speaking to Margaret LeVine. That would seem to contradict your statement. You do know that it's an offence to…'

'Okay, yes, stupid me, I should have said. We'd only run out of rosé, hadn't we? I don't drink the stuff, I only drink red, but Russell's got a taste for it. I nipped down to the High Street to get a bottle. I didn't really speak to Margaret: she just said hello or something like that. I was out and back in about 20 minutes, so I didn't think it was worth mentioning. Russell will back me up, once he's realised he needs to stop playing the knight in shining armour. I paid for the wine by card, so it'll be on my bank statement. You'll probably find me on the Waitrose CCTV too. I was back home before anything had happened. Or at least, if it happened while I was still there, I wasn't aware of it.'

Sutton looked over at Vicky to ask the next question, but she was staring into space. 'We'd like you to come into the station tomorrow and make a new statement,' he said to Dawson. 'A full and accurate one this time.'

'Tomorrow's not very convenient.'

'Neither is having the police arrive mob-handed to take you in and arrest you for wasting police time.'

'Just a sec,' said Vicky. 'I remember now. I was there when Margaret met you on the High Street and it's come back to me what she said to you.' She paused, seeing Sutton's expression.

'Could I speak to you privately for a moment,' Sutton said, gesturing towards the hall with his head.

'Okay. We won't be long, Ms Dawson.' Vicky followed Sutton out into the hall.

'I've read your statement,' Sutton whispered. 'You didn't mention hearing what LeVine said to people.'

'I said Miss LeVine had greeted a number of people. You're right, I didn't remember any details, but it's just come to me. Her name triggered a memory. You don't come across many Sukis, do you? Margaret told Dawson that she needed to see her that evening. I wonder what that was about?'

'Okay, but you need to amend your statement or Yaxley won't be the only one on the receiving end of the Inspector's tongue. Can you remember anyone else LeVine spoke to? This could be important evidence.'

Vicky shook her head. 'No, I can only remember this one because of the unusual name. I didn't know Margaret was going to be murdered, you know.'

'Sorry, I just don't want you ending up in the shit as well. Let's finish off.' Sutton led the way back into the sitting room.

'Sorry about that,' said Vicky to Dawson. 'We just

have one more question. As I said, I was present and just remembered what Margaret said to you. She told you that she needed to meet you that night. What was that about?'

Dawson looked down at her feet. 'Something and nothing. It was about festival finances. Just a small accounting issue.'

'It sounded more urgent than something and nothing. And you didn't think to tell us this?' asked Vicky.

'It didn't seem relevant,' said Dawson. 'It really wasn't important, but Margaret could be very fussy about small details.'

'Okay,' said Sutton. 'So, when you come to the station to make your amended statement tomorrow, could you bring any documents relevant to this accounting issue with you, please.'

'It'll take a day or two to get them together,' said Dawson.

'Okay,' said Sutton. 'That's fine. So how about ten am on Wednesday. Do we need to send a car for you?'

'No, no, I'll find my own way to the police station.'

'Perfect,' said Sutton. 'That would be perfect.'

CHAPTER 16

'Mr Levine – Russell – it's Detective Constable Denning here. It was good to see you on Friday. I do need to get in touch with you urgently. Please call me back as soon as you get this message.' Vicky hung up, scrunched up a ball of paper and threw it at Sutton, whose desk was nearly opposite hers. 'Still no joy from Levine. Have you tried his mobile provider?'

'Yeah,' said Sutton. 'He's not used his mobile since Friday. It's currently switched off. His last detected location was in the vicinity of his house.'

'We need to check if anyone's seen him,' said Vicky. 'Have we got time before the briefing?'

'Lots of time, it's been put off to Wednesday afternoon. Apparently both the boss and Crawford are off chasing something up. At least we'll have had the Dawson woman in by then, so something to report.'

'Er, there was the minor matter of Cherie Taylor's death.'

'Sorry, yes, that was thoughtless of me. Are you okay?'

'I'm fine. It was scary when we went in there, but after that it was more weird than anything. I mean, electromagnetic pulses? It's boys' toys stuff. I'm hoping Roland will have more for us soon.'

'Roland?'

'Mclean. The pathologist.'

'Friends?'

'More like family – he's my godfather.'

'Wow,' said Sutton. 'You come as a package, then?

I can see why they asked you over to help out.'

Vicky gave him her best hard stare. 'Any thoughts on who we can contact about the festival finances?'

'Only the committee. I don't know what else we can do. I'll work through the contact list and see what I can find.'

'Okay, I presume it's a charity, so there should be records. I'll check with the Charities Commission.'

Vicky pulled up the Commission's website and looked up the literature festival. 'Not bad finances,' she said. 'They seem to turn over around £50,000 a year.'

Sutton, with a phone tucked between his shoulder and chin nodded.

Clicking on Accounts and Annual Returns, Vicky pulled up the previous year's accounts for the festival and started to make notes.

Fifteen minutes later, Sutton put down the phone with a bang. 'I can't see we're going to get anything from that lot. As soon as I mentioned finances they clammed up. Said it was all down to LeVine and Dawson. Nothing to do with them.'

'Hmm,' said Vicky. 'The independent examiner is an accountant in Chippenham – I'll check with them, but the chances are it's just a box ticking exercise. These examiners aren't exactly forensic accountants. The only thing that seemed a bit odd to me was the level of trustees' expenses – things like accommodation and entertaining. It's been going up year on year, and by last year they were spending over £5,000 on it – that's a quite a lot for a £50,000 income. It makes you wonder whether some of that was spent on the entertainment of Ms Dawson.'

'Yep,' said Sutton. 'Something else to ask her when

we see her.'

Vicky's phone rang. 'Hi Roland, we were just talking about you.'

'Nothing bad, I hope,' said Mclean.

'Everything. All bad.'

'Hah. I was just ringing to confirm the cause of death for Cherie Taylor. Her pacemaker was fried, to use a technical term. It certainly wasn't just a technical failure – almost certainly it was caused by some kind of electromagnetic pulse device, though I'm having to wait for a technical expert to take a look to have solid evidence. There weren't any useful forensics from the body or the house – whoever did this was extremely careful.'

'Thanks, Roland.'

~

Wednesday morning, Vicky was back at Marlborough early. She met Sutton outside the station's only interview room. 'How long has she been here?'

'About half an hour,' said Sutton.

'She should be nicely twitchy, then.' Vicky pulled open the door and held it for Sutton. 'Good morning, Ms Dawson. I'll just start the recorder.'

While Sutton ran through the time and who was present, Vicky switched on the electronic recorder and opened a thick folder of paper she had carried in with her, all the while staring at Dawson, who looked suitably uncomfortable. Vicky had hoped that Dawson would say something unprompted, but the seconds passed and Dawson did not speak, her eyes lowered.

'Perhaps we can start with the festival finances,' said Vicky. 'I've taken a look at the annual reports.'

'Everything is audited; we have nothing to hide,' said Dawson. She did not look at Vicky.

'I notice that you spent around £5,000 on entertainment and accommodation for the last festival,' said Vicky.

'It's surely not normal to spend ten per cent of your income on that?' said Sutton.

Dawson glanced up at Sutton, still avoiding Vicky's eyes. 'It's not unusual, really. Book festivals always have a significant entertainment budget. We have to keep the authors happy – it's the least we can do, given we can't afford to pay them a going rate. And not many of them live nearby. We often have to put them up for the night. I can give you a breakdown.'

'That would be helpful,' said Vicky. 'Perhaps you could drop it off this afternoon. It went up a lot compared with the last year, didn't it? Who on the committee looked after the budget for entertainment and accommodation?'

Finally, Dawson looked at Vicky. 'That would be me.'

'And was that why Miss LeVine said she wanted to speak to you on the evening of her death? Had she concerns about the level of spending?'

'I'm guessing you've spoken to the other committee members. Okay, yes, she didn't like it: she thought it somehow made the festival feel more commercial, less folksy. But you've got to move with the times. I had no problem going through the details with her. If you heard her speak to me, you'll probably have heard me say that I couldn't see her that evening as I had a guest, but I'd see her the next day – Sunday. That's how we left it. Amicably. For

God's sake, I'm hardly going to kill the woman over spare change like a few thousand pounds.'

Vicky was conscious of Sutton staring at her. She closed her eyes for a moment, but could not remember Dawson's reply, just Margaret LeVine's words. 'We'll take your word for it for now. I also need to ask you about Russell Levine. Have you had any contact with Mr Levine since last Friday?'

Dawson shook her head. 'No, we aren't in constant communication, particularly when my husband is at home. Is that a problem?'

Vicky frowned. Dawson looked genuinely confused at the question. 'No, it's just that we're having trouble getting in touch with him. If you do hear from him, please let us know immediately.'

'We've checked the Waitrose CCTV as you suggested,' said Sutton. 'You were paying for your wine moments before the attack.'

'So that rules me out, doesn't it? I could hardly be paying for my Côtes de Provence and attacking Margaret at the same time.'

'When you got back to the house,' asked Vicky, 'where was Mr Levine?'

'What do you mean, where was he?'

'It's a simple enough question,' said Vicky. 'Which room was he in when you arrived back with your rosé wine? Did he greet you at the door?'

'He, er, I didn't see him straight away. I took the wine into the kitchen to stick it in the freezer for a few minutes. It wasn't cold enough. Russell came in from the back garden a minute or two later. He said he needed some fresh air. The house is lovely, but it can get stuffy when the central heating's on.'

'Okay,' said Vicky. 'Is the only access to your back

garden from the house?'

'No, there's a gate. It opens onto a footpath by the church that leads down onto Oxford Street. But I don't understand the relevance. I didn't use the back gate, I came in through the front door.'

'Thank you for your cooperation, Ms Dawson,' said Sutton. 'That will be all for now. If you can come with me, we'll just get a quick written statement and we're done.'

~

The doorbell sounded at exactly the same time that Capel's phone began to ring. It was Ed, on Facetime. Capel accepted the call and grinned at his friend. 'Hang on a second, Ed, someone at the door.' He jogged down the hall and opened the door to find three small children, dressed as a witch, a fairy and some sort of green monster. A woman he vaguely recognised from her occasional attendance at the children's service was hovering in the roadway behind them.

'Trick or treat!' the children called out, holding out little pumpkin-shaped baskets.

'I hope you don't mind,' said the woman, looking slightly embarrassed. 'I know it's not everyone's thing, you know, with the church and everything.'

Capel grinned. 'I don't know why people get so hung up about it, Halloween is a Christian tradition – it's here because it's All Saints' Day tomorrow.' He looked down at the children. 'Hang on.' Inwardly he thanked Vicky for having bought a tub of sweets, selling it to him on the argument that if no children came, as was common in the village – the evangelically oriented school discouraged their students from taking part – they could eat them all themselves.

'There you go, one each.' Capel let the children choose, smiled again at the woman and closed the door.

'Where's my sweet, then?' asked Ed.

Capel flipped his phone to the back camera and scanned it across the sweet tub. 'Help yourself.' Taking a sweet for himself and heading back to the kitchen, he switched the image back to his face. 'So, what do you think, now you've had a chance to look at the mystery document?' Capel tried to interpret Ed's expression, but his friend was at his most enigmatic.

'Hmm,' said Ed. 'It clearly is a code or cipher. The markings appear to be numbers, and they're grouped using brackets in a format that appears to be a key first number, then a pair of secondary numbers. I had a word with a colleague at GCHQ and she agreed with me that this is unlikely to be either a substitution or key cipher. Instead, I'd suggest that what we have here is a book cipher.'

'Does knowing that help us?'

'Yes… and no. A book cipher is both simple to use and impossible to crack without a vital piece of information. All you do is agree on a book to use, then look for the words that you want to put in your message within the book. When you locate a word, you simply write down the page number, line number and word number within the line. Strictly speaking you only need two numbers – the page and the position of the word within the page, but it usually takes a lot less effort to use line and word number in the line.'

'So it's easy to decipher?'

'Decode, I suppose, strictly. Ciphers substitute letter by letter, codes by word or phrase, so although it tends to be called a book cipher, it's really a code. Yes, it is easy to decode, as long as you know what the book is. That's the power of the approach. If you don't know the book – or even the correct edition of the book – then you haven't much hope. This document was written in 1885, wasn't it?'

'That's right.'

'Okay, that eliminates a huge number of books that have been published since then, but there were still plenty around. I've been doing my homework. These days, there are a couple of million new books published in English each year. Back in the 1880s, numbers were only in the low tens of thousands, but of course it wouldn't just be a matter of new books. As long as both sender and receiver had the same edition, the book itself could have been first written in Classical times. I've checked with your friends at the Cambridge University library, and they couldn't help with how many books our code writer had to choose from. Apparently, there were something like 30 or 40,000 individual editions available in English by the end of the fifteenth century, but they couldn't give a figure for the 1800s. Obviously a lot higher, though.'

'I suppose it's not something people often consider.'

'Mm. I gather from GCHQ that in that century in the UK, the most frequently used title for a book cipher was the Bible – though of course even with that, you had to agree on an edition. No surprise really. Just for a laugh, because that's the kind of people they are, they did check a few contemporary Bible editions, plus a number of the bestsellers of the period. Apparently, you could hardly move in the 1880s for books by someone called Margaret Oliphant – she pumped out at least one or two bestsellers a year. Trollope and Robert Louis Stephenson were good bets for the bestseller lists too. But they couldn't find anything meaningful from contemporary editions either.'

'How much government money has been spent on researching this for us?'

Ed winked. 'Don't ask. It's probably a more worthwhile piece of work than many of the things that GCHQ gets up to.'

'So, we need some way to discover exactly what the book was, or we're stuffed.'

'Indeed. "Stuffed" sums it up nicely.'

~

The following day, after picking up Capel from the evening All Saints' Day service, Vicky headed over to Marlborough, eventually pulling up her car in River Park, a back street parallel to the High Street. 'Are you sure this is it?' she said to Capel. 'It looks a bit… suburban for Miss LeVine's taste.'

'Snob,' said Capel. 'I admit I had envisaged some sort of ancient cottage with wisteria and such, but it's a handy location for the shops.'

'If the Kennet doesn't flood.' Vicky stepped out of the car. It was already dark and hard to make out the house numbers by the streetlights. 'What number was it?'

'Erm, 63, I think. Hang on.' Capel peered at his

phone. 'Yes, that's it.'

'Down the end there,' said Vicky. She led the way up the drive to a box-like red brick house, relatively modern but with little to distinguish it from its fellows in the road. Vicky took a set of keys from her pocket. The door opened to the second Yale key of the bunch.

'Are they hers?' asked Capel.

'Yes, according to the log we have two sets. These and a set we got off Russell Levine. He wasn't aware of any others. Here, put these on.' She handed Capel a pair of disposable gloves.

Capel pulled the gloves on and flicked on the hall light. 'It's warm in here.'

'The central heating must be going full blast.'

'You don't think of that,' said Capel. 'Making decisions when someone's dead. Who decides whether to leave it as it is or to turn it off?'

'Good question. If we come across a will, we might find out who to ask.' Vicky pointed to the thermostat further down the hallway. 'We could reasonably turn it down a bit. No need to keep it this hot.'

Capel nodded and turned the dial down from 23 to 18. 'So, where do we start? I'll be honest, it's mostly the church's book of myths and legends I'd like to get my hands on. It'd be a shame to lose it.'

'If you find it, bag it,' said Vicky, putting a small stack of evidence bags on the hall table. She pushed open the door into the lounge and peered in. 'At least it looks as if the place hasn't been turned over. I'll take a quick look upstairs. Don't move anything other than your book, but look for documents or anything that might seem relevant. Give me a shout if there's anything exciting.' She headed up the stairs.

Somewhat late for Vicky to see Capel nodded and switched on the lounge light. It was obvious at a glance that unless something was concealed, there was nothing worth looking at in there. The room was comfortably furnished, but there was not a single book or scrap of paper. It was not entirely surprising. A full-time writer would most likely have some kind of study to work in. He had just established that the only other ground floor rooms were the kitchen and dining room, plus a small cloakroom, when there was a sharp rap on the front door.

'Vicky? There's someone at the door.'

'Can you answer it,' she shouted down. 'I'm up to my elbows in drawers.'

Capel felt there had to be a witty answer to that, but it didn't come to mind quickly enough. He pulled open the front door to see a grey-haired man with a moustache that curled up at both ends in a dramatic fashion. 'Hello, can I help you?' Capel said.

'My wife is ready to call the police if I don't return home in ninety seconds,' said the man.

'Erm, right,' said Capel.

'Who are you, and what are you doing in Miss LeVine's house?'

'Ah. I'm here with the police. Hang on.' Capel turned to the stairs. 'Vicky! Now, please.'

Vicky came rattling down the stairs.

'This gentleman wants to know who we are and why we're here.'

Vicky took out her warrant card and held it up, only to have it pulled from her grasp. 'Detective Constable Denning,' she said. 'Investigating the death of Margaret LeVine. And you are?'

'I am a, er, neighbour. I was concerned that someone was in the house illegally. My wife…'

Vicky had pulled out her notebook. 'Name?'

'Judith.'

Vicky tried to conceal a laugh in a cough. 'Your name.'

'Sorry. Victor Rundle. I live across there at number 58. We're Neighbourhood Watch, you see.'

'Of course you are,' said Vicky. 'And an excellent job you're doing too. If you don't mind, though, we need to get on.'

'Naturally, naturally. I should get back to Judith anyway. She was supposed to call the police if I wasn't back by now.' He gestured towards his house, where the curtain was twitching.

'Thank you for your concern,' said Vicky. 'Erm, my warrant card?'

'Sorry, sorry,' said Rundle, handing it over.

Capel closed the door. 'I suppose you can't really complain.'

Vicky shook her head. 'Found anything?'

'Not yet. There's no study or office down here. Is she using one of the bedrooms to write in?'

'Nope. There's just a master bedroom, and a couple of spares. One a guest room, the other rigged out as a home gym. I would never have taken Margaret for the home gym type.'

'We all have our little foibles,' said Capel. 'So where did she write? Where are all her books and papers?'

'When I was a kid, we went on a school trip to the Roald Dahl museum. You know, in Great Missenden in Buckinghamshire. He lived there for years and wrote his children's books in the village. The museum isn't his house – I think it used to be a coaching inn – but it's got lots of his stuff, including the inside of his writing hut. I think quite a lot of writers have something in the garden where they work, to get away from things.'

'Good thinking, detective constable. Let's check out the garden.'

It took Vicky a couple of goes to find the key to the back door. Capel pressed the light switch alongside the door and turned off the kitchen light. 'Sorry, thought it might be an outside light.' Once he had the light back on, he saw a second switch on the other side of the door. 'There we go.'

'Oh, yes,' said Vicky.

At the bottom of the garden was a huge shed spanning the entire width of the garden. It even had a wooden veranda with a table and chairs. 'I want one of those,' said Capel.

'You haven't even got a house of your own,' said Vicky. 'It's a bit ambitious to want a garden retreat.'

'Fair point. But I still want one.'

The shed had a sophisticated lock, and when Vicky opened the door with one of the keys, an alarm started to beep. 'Oh bugger,' she said. She grabbed a torch from her pocket and shone it on the alarm panel just inside the door.

'Any idea?' said Capel, peering at the panel. 'What's her date of birth?'

Vicky looked through her notebook. 'Sixth of July, 1953.'

Capel tried every combination he could think of. 'Nope. We've got another 20 seconds apparently. Eighteen… have you got Russell's birthday?'

Vicky shook her head. 'Not with me. Hang on, it's

February 29th, I remember now, he told me. Don't know what year, though.'

Capel quickly keyed in 0229 and the alarm light glowed green. 'We're in.'

Vicky grinned. 'Just as well, or we'd no doubt have Captain Neighbourhood Watch back to check up on us.' She turned on the lights inside the shed. There was an elegant corner desk with a large computer screen, a pair of filing cabinets, two full height cupboards and thousands of books in shelves that ran around every available square foot of wall space.

'Wow,' said Capel. 'This is going to take a bit of searching.'

Vicky nodded. 'Have a look at the desk and the cupboards. I'll try the filing cabinets. At some point, someone is going to have to look through all those books, but I'm hoping that it's not going to be me.'

Capel sat down in the chair in front of the desk and flicked through papers in a stack by the computer. There was nothing obviously relevant – the paperwork seemed to be mostly receipts and invoices for filing. He pulled open the top drawer of a three-drawer unit below the desk. It was entirely full of glasses cases. He counted over twenty. The second drawer had an eclectic mix – Victorian postcards, a guide to Hampton Court Palace… he recognised the copy of the Anglo-Saxon Chronicle that Miss LeVine had brought with her when they met. And beneath it was nestled the church's battered leatherbound notebook. 'I've got the book,' he said.

'Excellent,' said Vicky. 'Hang on.'

Capel picked up the notebook and flicked through it, feeling that his blue-plastic covered hands made it feel like watching something in a TV drama. He had glanced at the notebook before when he first arrived in the parish, but he couldn't really remember a lot of what was in it. The notes were written in several different hands, clearly added to over the years as local legends had been passed down. He spotted the king of cats one that Peter had mentioned. The back few pages were blank, but when he turned to the very last page it had a list of churchwardens who had contributed to the contents, starting with a Joshua Barton in 1794.

'There's a will here,' said Vicky.

Capel put the book face down on one of the evidence bags and turned the chair to face her. 'Anything interesting?'

'It's very short. Nothing fancy, no specific bequests. She's left everything to Russell, lock, stock and barrel.'

'Does that count as a motive?'

Vicky did something with her nose that Capel had never quite known how to describe, but that usually indicated scepticism. 'She's no J. K. Rowling. It's a nice enough house, but I doubt if she's exactly rolling in it. I can't remember the numbers, but when they checked her bank statements, it was all pretty pedestrian. Don't get me wrong, people have been murdered for a lot less, but it's not what you'd call a heavy-duty motive, especially for someone like Russell Levine.'

'Hmm.' Capel picked up the notebook. 'I don't know if she ever got a chance to look at the notebook, but it's quite interesting. When I looked at it a few years ago, I never got as far as the back page, because quite a lot of it towards the back is blank. Look, there's a list of contributors. The oldest one's over 220 years ago. Joshua Barton, Benjamin Unwin, James East, William Spencer, Basil Christie and another James, James Smith.'

'Not a lot of women. As in none.'

'Not surprising, the way they tended to choose churchwardens back then. They're all churchwardens as far as I can gather. They often took an interest in local history.'

'Hmm. Stick it in a bag and let's get on.'

'Okay. Has this place already been searched?'

'It should have been ages ago, but there was nothing logged – I've been waiting for another explosion from the Inspector. Why?'

Capel poked the papers on top of the desk with his gloved finger. 'I thought there was something funny about these, and I've just realised what. This looks like piling to me.'

'What?'

'Pile filing. It's quite a clever technique. Rather than taking the time to sort things and file them conventionally, you put them in a pile and move a document to the top if and when you use it. So, the stuff you need frequently is always near the top. But that apart, you tend to get the older stuff at the bottom. This was the other way up. Oldest stuff on top. As if…'

'Someone's been through them.'

Capel nodded.

'It's possible. Like I said, a team should have been over everything already, though to be honest, with no one living here, I'd expect things to be left in a bit more of a mess after a routine search. I'll check next time I'm in the station at Marlborough.'

Capel looked through the remaining drawers, but

nothing leapt out. He realised he had really only been looking for the notebook. One of the cupboards was fully of copies of Margaret's books, the other held stationery.

Vicky pushed the bottom file drawer closed with a slam. 'Nothing else obvious. I'll note it as a first line inspection, in case no one has been here before. Which of course they should have been. Remember what Suki Dawson said about Margaret's platform to be P and CC. She had a point – some of the Marlborough lot are less than ideal.'

'Except for the blessed Jamie.'

'I only said some. The inspector and Alicia Crawford – and, yes, Jamie – they are all great. But that Yaxley guy, for example, is total deadwood. I suspect this was another of his failures.'

Capel slipped the notebook into an evidence bag. 'If someone checks this over and there's nothing significant, could I have it back? I'd quite like to read it properly.'

'Of course – if no one else apart from Margaret touched it, I can't see there's a problem. This place isn't short of books. I mean, technically it's still evidence, but as long as it's logged and checked by forensics, it should be okay. I'll take it in tomorrow, you can have a proper look at it tomorrow night.'

CHAPTER 17

'Right, boys and girls.' Inspector Davis seemed to be in a particularly sunny mood for a Monday morning. 'What have we learned since our last little get-together? Crawford?'

The sergeant took a long drink from her mug. 'Nothing helpful from the CCTV. A number of the persons of interest were present at the Mop – no surprise there – but we couldn't pick up anything that looked suspicious.'

Davis flicked a picture of Cherie Taylor onto the big screen, looking pleased with himself for managing this without help. 'Quick summary on our second victim?'

'Denning?' said Crawford.

'As you know, we had a call from her and attended her house as the call was interrupted. She was dead when we arrived. The pathologist believes that her pacemaker was damaged intentionally using some sort of electromagnetic pulse device. Other electronic technology in the house was also destroyed.'

'That sounds pretty high tech,' said Davis. 'Could anyone get hold of one of these pulse devices?'

Vicky shook her head. 'The official line is that small portable EMP devices don't exist. I checked with a Home Office contact. Apparently, MI5 mislaid one about four years ago – but it seems unlikely it would have ended up in Melksham.'

'Okay. Why Taylor?' asked Davis. 'Anyone?'

'She must have known something about the murder,' said DC Sutton. 'I suppose she even could have done it, and this was revenge.'

'It's not impossible, but it feels implausible,' said Davis. 'Did she say anything when you spoke to her on the phone, Denning?'

Vicky shook her head. 'I told her we'd been trying to get in touch, she explained how she liked to go off the grid when she was writing a book, and then things started happening.'

Davis nodded. He flicked through on his tablet to the priority action list. 'Please tell me that the search of Margaret LeVine's house hasn't been missed. Yaxley?'

The former detective constable pulled uncomfortably at his uniform jacket. 'It's not me, guv. I've been on paperwork since the other thing.'

'Sorry,' said Sutton. 'It has been done – I did it a couple of days ago – but it's not logged yet. It was overtaken by events. Nothing much to report, apart from a will leaving everything to the nephew. No threatening letters, nothing about a dispute with anyone.'

'Sir,' said Vicky, conscious she had been operating without authority the previous night, 'I did call in at LeVine's myself yesterday. I hadn't realised DC Sutton had already been. It wasn't a comprehensive search, though I saw the will too. We, erm, I was hoping to retrieve this.' She held up the evidence bag with the church notebook in it.

'And this is what exactly?' said Davis.

'It's a collection of myths and legends that Miss LeVine borrowed from Thornton Down church. The vicar was concerned it appeared to have gone missing. I've had it checked – there are no prints on it except the vicar's and Miss LeVine's. Swabs have been taken for DNA, but it has no obvious bearing. Is there any problem once logged if I return it to the church? It wasn't Miss LeVine's property.'

'I suppose not,' said Davis. 'Anything else, people?'

'I've finally got to speak to someone at BAFTA,' said Crawford. 'About LeVine's agent, Norman Fox. It seems that Mr Fox was telling us porkies. He had an invitation to attend the event there, but he never signed in.'

'Okay,' said Davis. 'I think it's time we got serious with Mr Fox. Get uniform to bring him in.'

'From London?' said Crawford.

'The budget can stretch to it. I want you to get him off home turf. Might encourage him to be cooperative.'

'Will do, boss.'

'And ask him about her politics as well. Wasn't there something about that in one of your reports, Denning?' asked Davis.

'That's right,' said Vicky, flicking through her notebook. 'Ms Dawson told us that Miss LeVine had stood for Police and Crime Commissioner, but she didn't make it.'

Davis groaned. 'Much though I'd like to see the back of our new incumbent, I can't see him wiping out the opposition after he'd won the election. One thing we all know about Police and Crime Commissioners is that very few people care about them. What's the news on Mr Levine?'

'Still haven't been able to contact him, guv,' said Sutton. 'No one has seen him since DC Denning met him the other Friday.'

'Denning?' Davis stared at Vicky.

'He was fine then,' she said. 'We just took a look a couple of sites that Margaret LeVine had wanted to visit. But I am getting concerned that he hasn't responded to our messages.'

'Okay, no need to panic at this stage, but Sergeant Crawford could you get someone to check his house and workplace? If he hasn't surfaced since Denning spoke to him, and there's no sign, I think we need a warrant to check his place over.'

Crawford nodded at Sutton. 'Can you get onto that?'

Davis nodded, not waiting for Sutton's agreement. 'And how about Ms Dawson? She was brought in for interview?'

'That's right,' said Sutton. 'She had misled us about her whereabouts on the night LeVine was killed. Dawson did seem to have a minor falling out with Miss LeVine over festival finances, but it seems unlikely to be significant. Perhaps more interesting, she – Dawson, I mean – was having a cosy evening in with Russell Levine the night of Miss LeVine's death.'

'So she has given him an alibi?' asked Crawford.

'No, she can't,' said Vicky. 'Dawson went out to buy some wine. We've got her on CCTV in Waitrose at the time of the killing. But when she got back, Russell Levine wasn't in the house. He came in shortly afterwards from the back garden, which opens onto a convenient path leading down to the High Street. He said he'd just been getting some fresh air. He has no alibi at the moment.'

'That's very interesting,' said Davis. 'All the more reason to track him down. Anything else, anyone?'

Everyone looked down at the table or shook their heads. 'Fair enough. Looks like we have no new suspects, with Levine as highest priority right now. Let's go back over what we have got. Check everything again. Speak to the other persons of interest as well as Fox again. Something, somewhere, is going to give us a way in.'

Davis headed back to his office. As Vicky picked up her notebook from the table, Sergeant Crawford touched her arm. 'Vicky, got a moment?'

'Yes, sarge.'

'I've told you, Alicia is fine. We've got that agent, Norman Fox, due in for an interview. Want to sit in with me?'

'Of course.'

Fox was already in the interview room when Vicky followed Crawford in. The sergeant started the voice recorder and identified those present.

'Is this necessary?' asked Fox, his tone petulant. 'It's a long way to come for a chat. They have this amazing thing called a telephone now.'

'I'm afraid so,' said Crawford. 'We need to clear up some significant points, Mr Fox. Could you remind us where you were at the time that Margaret LeVine was killed? Say between 6pm and 9pm on the night of Saturday the seventeenth of October.'

'I already told this young lady,' said Fox. 'I was attending an event at BAFTA. It's in Piccadilly, you know. I was there all evening.'

'And how about Friday the twenty-third of October?'

'Why?'

'We're just trying to sort out a timeline on some associated events,' said Vicky. 'It's routine.'

'Just a moment. I'm a busy man. Can't always know where I've been of the top of my head.' Fox pulled out his pocket diary and leafed through. 'Oh, yes. I was having a pamper day at the spa. Bulgari in Knightsbridge. Sometimes, one simply needs to unwind.'

'We'll check that out,' said Crawford. 'But for the moment let's go back to the seventeenth of October. The event at BAFTA. We've checked with the people there, and unfortunately it seems that you didn't turn up.'

'That's outrageous,' said Fox. 'I'm a member. They should be more discreet about our comings and goings.'

'This is a murder enquiry, Mr Fox.'

Fox sniffed. 'Look, I simply didn't want to waste your time. Yes, in the end I didn't go, but I had intended to do so, and I didn't go anywhere else instead. I was at home, alone before you ask.'

'All evening?' asked Vicky.

'Yes. Well, except for when I went out.'

Crawford raised her eyebrows. 'Could you amplify on that?'

'I left my flat twice that evening. Once to the off licence to get some whisky and once to the local corner shop to buy some food.'

'Do you know what time those visits took place?' asked Crawford.

'No.'

'Just roughly,' said Vicky. 'To the nearest hour, say.'

'I suppose. I bought the whisky about six o'clock and the food around seven. A frozen meal for one, if you must know. Allegedly beef stroganoff.'

'Do you think they'll have CCTV in the shops?' asked Crawford.

A FAIR DELIVERANCE

'It's London,' said Fox. 'Of course they will.'

'It might be deleted by now,' said Vicky.

'But it tends to be kept longer now it's mostly digital,' said Crawford. 'Which off licence and shop are we talking about, Mr Fox?'

'You expect me to know their names?' said Fox. 'I don't read the signs, I just go in.'

'Don't worry,' said Crawford, 'DC Denning will show you a map and you can retrace your steps for us. Denning?'

'On it,' said Vicky. She hurried out of the interview room and picked up an iPad, bringing up Google Maps, and took it back in.

'Remind me of your home address, Mr Fox,' said Vicky.

'Bickenhall Mansions,' said Fox. 'Number 83.'

'Sounds very grand,' said Vicky. She pulled up the address on the iPad. 'Can you show me where you go?'

Fox pointed at the map. 'Up Baker Street here and across the Marylebone Road. The off licence is just there.'

'I see it,' said Crawford. 'One Stop. I see it says it's a food shop too. But you went somewhere else to buy something to eat?'

'The off licence is overpriced,' said Fox. 'But they have a better choice of whisky than the plebs at Tesco Express, which is where I went for food. In Baker Street, that one is.'

'Thanks, Mr Fox,' said Vicky.

'And you are sure you didn't speak to anyone else?' asked Crawford.

'No,' said Fox. 'Are we finished?'

'For the moment,' said Crawford. 'Are you okay to

see yourself out?'

'The sooner the better,' said Fox. 'I'll just get myself an Uber to get back to the railway station.' He slammed out of the interview room.

'Do you think we should have told him there aren't Ubers in Marlborough?' Vicky asked.

'He'll find out soon enough,' said Crawford. 'Could you chase up the CCTV from those shops. You might have to get the local station to go round and copy it, but if you sound assertive enough, some of these places'll just email it to you.'

~

It was several hours later that Sutton arrived back in the team room.

'How'd it go?' asked Vicky.

'Nothing to suggest where Levine is,' said Sutton. 'There was no phone, but if he's taken clothes with him, he's left plenty behind. His passport was there, but I guess if he's gone on the run, he'd try to get hold of a fake. The most worrying thing was his cat.'

'What about his cat?' asked Vicky.

'It was dead. Looked starved. Lots of scratching about the place. Poor thing was emaciated. All skin and bone. The woodentop I had with me nearly threw up.'

'So maybe Russell didn't leave voluntarily. That's worrying. Was there anything to link him to the murders?'

'There was this.' Sutton dropped an evidence bag with a sheet of A4 paper in it on Vicky's desk.

She picked up the paper. It was a printout from the internet. A page on EMP devices. 'Interesting. But nothing more concrete?'

'This was quite interesting.' He dropped a smaller evidence bag on the desk, containing a yellow Post-it note. On it was written Cherie Taylor's address.

'Wow. Why would he have her address?'

'Why indeed. He's looking pretty dodgy. The techies have got his laptop: we'll have to see if there are any clues to his whereabouts there. He can't hide forever. How about you?'

'Alicia and I spoke to Norman Fox, Margaret LeVine's agent.'

'Alicia is it? All girls together now?'

'Piss off. The sarge is okay. Fox admitted he'd lied, apparently to save us all from having to waste our time. But he was in an off licence at 6.15pm and a Tesco Express at just after 7pm. There's no way he could have got here in time to kill Margaret.'

'Unless he lied about that too.'

Vicky shook her head. 'Not this time. With a little help from our friends in the Met, we've got CCTV placing him in those shops. He's a pain in the arse, but he didn't kill her.'

CHAPTER 18

A month passed with no news on the murders. Vicky started to spend less time in Marlborough. There was no trace of Russell Levine and a limit to the options left open to the team. In Thornton Down, Capel was working on the parish website when the doorbell rang. Websites and social media might be considered necessary for a parish these days, but dealing with them was not his favourite occupation – he shut the computer with a smile on his face.

On the doorstep he found an unfamiliar couple, a short plump man with thinning yellow hair and a long beard, accompanied by a much taller woman whose hair was an impressively vivid shade of purple. At least their jeans and t-shirts – seemingly offering far too little protection for the cold winter morning – showed they weren't Jehovah's Witnesses. On occasion he enjoyed a good biblical debate on his doorstep, but he wasn't in the mood for it today. 'Hello. Can I help you?'

'Well, yeah vicar,' said the man. 'We were told you were the man when it came to significant locations in these parts.' He winked.

The woman sighed. 'I'm sorry, I'm Sandy, this is Rob. We wondered if we could have a minute of your time. It's about local archaeology.'

'I can't claim to be an expert,' said Capel, 'but I'm happy to have a chat. Come in.' He took them into the sitting room and made some tea for them. 'So, what's this about,' he said as he bought a tray with the mugs and small pile of biscuits on into the room.

'We're detectorists,' said the woman. 'I know people think it's a bit like being a trainspotter. People think we're a joke, just cos they think it's childish, hunting for treasure and that. But using metal detectors is a proper hobby.'

'I'm sure it is,' said Capel. 'But if you're going to ask to hunt in our graveyard, I'm afraid I'm going to have to decline. The diocese has very strict rules on this. You have to remember we're in the business of burying bodies, not treasure.'

'Oh no, no,' said the man. 'It's about somewhere else entirely.'

Capel shook his head. 'I don't really see, then, where I come in. I don't have jurisdiction anywhere else. If it's the school you want permission from, you need to speak to the bursar, I'd imagine.'

'It's not a matter of permission, and it's a bit sensitive,' said the woman. 'We were contacted by a Margaret LeVine about finding possible buried artefacts for her. She said she was coming to see you to get help on the location. And we haven't been able to get in touch with her, so we thought you might know…'

'I'm sorry,' said Capel. 'I am afraid Miss LeVine is dead.'

'Oh. Oh, dear. We had no idea.' The man, Rob, seemed to be struggling to come up with the right facial expression, settling on something that suggested he had toothache rather than sympathy.

'That is a shock,' said Sandy. 'I don't want to seem heartless, but do you happen to know where it was that Miss LeVine wanted us to search? She never went into any details about the location and it feels like it would be a tribute to her if we made the search anyway.'

'Okay,' said Capel. 'Look, I'm really sorry, but I've got to go out in a moment.' He pulled out his phone and checked his diary. 'Are you available tomorrow? No, erm, Wednesday.'

'Of course,' said Sandy.

'That's great,' said Capel. 'Sorry, Sandy and Rob what?' He took a scrap of paper and a pen off the mantlepiece.

'Savage,' said Rob. 'Savage by name and…'

'Shut up, Rob,' said Sandy.

Capel took their number and saw them out. He picked up the phone and dialled.

Vicky was driving into Marlborough when Capel's name came up on her phone. 'Hello dearest,' she said.

'Hi. Where are you?'

'Heading over to Marlborough.'

'I thought they'd run out of things for you to do?'

'It's certainly running down, but I've got a morning over here today. I told you last night.'

'You probably did. I just wanted to talk to you about a couple of rather strange visitors I've just had. Connected to Margaret.'

'Important?'

'I'm really not sure.'

'Okay, I'll call you when I can – otherwise, take me through it tonight.'

~

After a morning in Marlborough, Vicky was sitting at her desk back in the Bath police station, contemplating her less than exciting lunchtime sandwich and wondering if she could justify getting a burger instead.

Her phone rang – an unfamiliar number. 'Hello, DC Denning.'

'Good afternoon. It's Doctor Schmidt here at the University Library.'

'Hello, how can I help you?'

'You asked me to let you know if someone else enquired about the Combe Down brooch document that you examined.'

Vicky put down her sandwich and grabbed her notebook. 'Yes, please. When was this?'

'I got an email requesting a scan of the document this morning. It was, erm, yes, from your colleague at Marlborough police station. It's an official police email address, so I saw no problem…'

'No, of course,' said Vicky. 'It was to be expected, just to get official confirmation. But I'd still be grateful if you could let me know if anyone else ask about it in the future.'

'Of course,' said Schmidt. 'I'm sorry, I'm very pushed for time, if you will excuse me.' She hung up.

Just as Vicky picked up her sandwich again, the phone rang again. Capel. 'Hi gorgeous,' Vicky said. 'Say something to cheer me up.'

'My mind has gone totally blank,' said Capel. 'You're off tomorrow, aren't you?'

'Yep. Forty-eight glorious hours without having to think about work.'

'Ah,' said Capel. 'Of course, in my job you're always on duty. And it's true of police officers really too, isn't it?'

'Why? Be very careful what you say next.'

Capel sighed. 'I've been thinking a bit more about those visitors I mentioned earlier. an odd couple, who may have a connection to the LeVine case.'

Vicky carefully put down her sandwich again, stared at it for a moment then threw it in the bin. Fate clearly intended her not to eat it. 'Right, you've got my interest.'

'Names Rob and Sandy Savage. Detectorists, apparently. You know, metal detectors, hunting for treasure and finding old bottle tops. Like that TV show. I thought they were just your standard vicarage-visiting cranks. We do get them from time to time.'

'But?'

'Apparently they'd been asked by Margaret LeVine to help search for treasure of some sort. They claimed that they didn't know she was dead, but also said that they were trying to find out where Margaret wanted them to search, because they intended to go ahead and make the search anyway, as a kind of memorial. I didn't feel it was fair at this point to mention the inconsistency between the two parts of the story. Thought I'd leave it to the professionals. They're coming back on Wednesday.'

'Oh, joy,' said Vicky. 'No, actually, it sounds interesting. It's a possible motive.'

'Yes,' said Capel slowly. 'I'll be honest, they don't strike me as the kind to carry out a sophisticated attack like the one at the Mop. But someone certainly needs to talk to them.'

'You're right. I'll have a word with the sergeant at Marlborough and see what she says.'

~

With a slight feeling of déjà vu, Capel showed Rob and Sandy Savage into the sitting room. 'Nice to see you again,' he said. 'Could I introduce you to my fiancée, Vicky and her friend Alicia.'

'Well, hello,' said Rob, looking suddenly significantly more cheerful.

Sandy curled her lip at him. 'This is very kind of you, Mr erm... We don't want to take up too much of your time, but it really would be helpful to know where Margaret was hoping to search.' She opened a voluminous handbag and pulled an Ordnance Survey map, unfolding it on her knee and turning it so it was the right way up for Capel to see. She pointed at Thornton Down. 'This is where we are now. Could you show us where it is Miss LeVine wanted to search?'

'Before we get onto that,' said Alicia Crawford, 'we probably should introduce ourselves in a little more detail. Capel said you were Rob and Sandy?'

'Savage,' said Sandy.

'Savage by name and...' Rob stopped with a hurt expression as Sandy hit his leg with a sound like a whipcrack.

'Thank you,' said Crawford. 'I am Detective Sergeant Alicia Crawford. This is Detective Constable Victoria Denning.' They each produced a warrant card.

'So, when the Reverend said you were his fiancée, it was crap,' said Sandy.

'No, I am his fiancée as well,' said Vicky.

'We would like to ask you a few questions pertaining to the deaths of Margaret LeVine and Cherie Taylor,' said Crawford.

'Who?' asked Rob Savage. 'Like we said, we're here because Margaret asked us to get involved, but I don't know Cherie Taylor.'

Vicky glanced at her notebook. 'Could you tell us where you were on the night of Saturday the seventeenth of October?'

'How would I know?' asked Rob. 'I don't even know where I was last weekend.'

Sandy pulled a battered phone out of the backpack by her feet. 'Shut up, Rob.' She flicked at the screen. 'We were at a detectorists' event in Taunton, weren't we? I was speaking at it. I'm well-known in the community. You can see on the website. There are pictures and everything, only I haven't got decent reception here.'

'Have you got a laptop we could use?' Crawford asked Capel.

'Of course.' Capel brought his computer in and let Sandy search for the site.

'Here,' she said, turning the laptop around so the others could see the screen.

Vicky took it and scrolled through the page. 'It looks genuine. The date and time is right and they're both in the photographs from the event. We'd have to check with the organisers, but they look to be in the clear.'

'How about Friday the twenty-third of October?' asked Crawford. 'Around lunchtime.'

Sandy consulted her phone again. 'At the supermarket, I'd imagine. There'd be CCTV.'

'I'll take the details off you later,' said Vicky. 'Could I ask you about when you heard about Miss LeVine's death? Reverend Capel says that you originally showed surprise that she was dead, but then suggested you were visiting to find information to do a hunt in memory of Miss LeVine. It can't be both.'

Sandy sighed. 'Yes, okay, it was stupid. As I like to

call my husband. It was his idea. We read about Margaret and it was obvious she was after some sort of treasure, so it seemed a shame to let it go to waste. Only it seemed a bit money grubbing if we said we knew and that was the reason we'd come looking.'

'Oh, it did seem a bit money grubbing,' said Crawford. 'It really did.'

~

When Vicky came in on Christmas Eve, Capel was hunting through the wall of bookcases in his study.

'Looking for inspiration for your Christmas Day sermon?'

Capel smiled. 'Hi. No, hunting up a suitably Christmassy murder mystery. I've always enjoyed them this time of year. Nothing too gruesome, of course. But for some reason mysteries and ghost stories always go well this time of year. How was work?'

'Fairly tedious. Mostly dealing with the traditional Christmastime pastimes of theft and burglary. There hasn't been anything for weeks on the LeVine case. I'm not sure that one's going anywhere. How about you?'

Capel smiled. 'Well, the Christingle service was its usual chaotic fun. But no one got set on fire, which is always a plus.' He checked his watch. 'And I've only got half an hour before I need to get ready for the Midnight Mass. I know it doesn't start until 11.30, but people arrive really early for Christmas services. That's why I wanted to get my bedtime reading sorted. Ah-hah!' He pulled a black hardback from the shelves. 'Here we go, *Midwinter Murder*. It's Agatha Christie short stories. Ideal stuff…' A thought occurred to him: 'No relation to the churchwarden.' At the same time, Vicky said 'I wonder if the man behind the brooch letter was related.'

'Agatha Christie was born in the west country,' said Capel, 'but she was from Devon, I think, so unlikely to be related to our churchwarden Basil…' His voice trailed off. 'Brooch letter? Have you still got the picture of the documentation for the brooch?'

'Yes, hang on.' Vicky pulled out her phone and flicked through the images. 'Here.'

Capel stretched the image to see the name Basil Christie, then went over to his desk where the leather notebook of legends was lying. He opened it at the back to the list of contributors. 'Bloody hell, it looks like our Basil is the same Basil as that Basil, if you see what I mean.' He slumped into his office chair.

Vicky pulled off her shoes and sat in the only other chair in the study. 'So the guy who found the Anglo-Saxon brooch was a churchwarden in Thornton Down, and he wrote some of the legends up.'

'More than that, maybe,' said Capel. 'Can you read out the number symbols at the bottom of the brooch document for me?' He grabbed a piece of paper and a pen.

'Sure,' said Vicky. 'It's 5 (2,2), then 20 (13, 5), then 1 (4, 4), then 36 (8, 2), then 9 (11, 3), then 11 (6, 1), then 29 (2, 9) and finally 51 (10, 4). You don't think…?'

'I do think,' said Capel. The notebook pages weren't numbered, so he counted forward to page five, then handed Vicky the paper and pen. 'Read them out to me one at a time, and note down the words.'

'Okay, first it's 5 (2,2).'

'That's the number 100.'

'Then 20 (13, 5).'

'Hang on, page 20… that's "paces" – 100 paces – Basil clearly was fond of reading pirate novels. The Victorians loved them for some reason.'

Vicky worked her way through the locations as Capel built the phrase.

'Right, so we have "100 paces from the south entrance sub rosa." I think we've cracked it.'

'What's with the bit at the end?' Vicky asked.

'Sub rosa? Literally it means under the rose in Latin – it usually refers to a secret, something that's confidential. So, it's telling us the secret location is 100 paces from the south entrance.'

'Or could it be literal?'

'What do you mean?'

'A pace is a notoriously inaccurate measurement, even if it's the same person, let alone if someone else tries to reproduce it. So surely Basil will have left some sort of marker?'

'In the form of a rose. Good thinking – very elegant. It's like one of those really good crossword clues, when you get it, it's convincing. Sub rosa with the double meaning of a secret and being hidden under the image of the rose.'

'Shall we go and look?' asked Vicky.

'Erm, vicar here, Christmas Eve. Also, it's only around 36 hours to our wedding. Whatever's there, if there's anything there at all, it has been waiting over a thousand years. I think it can hold on a few more. And for that matter, it's not going to be a matter of just digging a hole in some soil. The tunnel is paved and mostly lined with brick. It's going to take serious scanning – something like ground penetrating radar – and proper excavation. This isn't a job for amateurs like those detectorists.'

'Fair enough,' said Vicky.

Capel glanced at his watch. 'Now, are you coming to the Midnight? It has always been one of my favourite services. For some reason it combines something very special spiritually, and atmospheric with all the candles, with a comfortable lack of formality. Perhaps it's the way the choir turns up in their Christmas jumpers.'

Vicky frowned. 'I won't, if you don't mind. I need to get everything ready to go over to mum's flat after dinner tomorrow and I need to catch up on my beauty sleep.

~

With the Christmas morning service out of the way, Capel was able to switch out of vicar mode and get working on the vegetables in the kitchen. Vicky had put the turkey in earlier and the aromas were already enticing.

An hour later, Vicky's phone rang just as she was pouring fizzy wine into orange juice to make a second glass of Buck's Fizz. 'Can you get it?' she shouted through to Capel, who was setting the table. 'I wouldn't want to interrupt the pouring of alcohol.'

'Fair enough,' said Capel. 'Vicky Denning's phone?'

'Morning, Capel, and Happy Christmas.'

'Same to you, Roland.' Capel put his hand over the phone. 'It's the godfather. He's not coming here for Christmas dinner, is he?'

'Not that I know of,' said Vicky. 'I was only

expecting the two of us, but to be honest, there's enough here to feed a football team.'

'It's weird,' said Capel. 'Having Christmas without family. I mean, except us, given we're almost family… maybe I should stop digging.'

'Perhaps you could ask him?'

'Sorry?'

'Roland. Waiting on the phone.'

'Shit.' Capel put the phone back to his ear. 'Sorry about that, Roland, I was being distracted by your goddaughter. What are you plans for today?'

'Erm, I've got a friend coming over,' said Mclean.

'A friend? Do I know him? Or her?'

'Well, erm,' the pathologist sounded uncharacteristically flustered. 'Perhaps. Probably. Anyway, I was ringing with some news. I've been called out to a body.'

'On Christmas Day? There really is no rest for the wicked.'

'No, yesterday, but I knew you'd a lot on. It's Russell Levine.'

'He's dead?'

'Bodies usually are.'

'Just a sec,' said Capel, 'I'm putting you on speaker. Vicky's here.'

'Happy Christmas, Vic!' said Mclean.

'Hope you're having a good one,' said Vicky. 'Who's dead?'

'He's got a friend coming over,' said Capel, winking. 'And apparently it's Russell Levine.'

'Really? Russell Levine's going to Roland for Christmas dinner?'

'Levine's dead,' said Capel.

'Where? How? When?'

'You need to hone your interrogation skills, Detective Constable Denning,' said Mclean. 'One question at a time always works well. Yes, Savernake Forest, a shotgun and he was found yesterday but had been dead some time. It's too early to give anything near a precise time period, but given the state of the body, I'd say he died shortly after he disappeared at the end of October.'

'And when you say shotgun?' asked Vicky.

'Close quarters. A good approximation to suicide.'

'Approximation?'

'Again, it's too early to be definitive, but the apparent angle doesn't work for me. Give me a few days. It is a bank holiday, you know.'

'We've been busy too,' said Vicky. 'We decoded the message on the brooch document. It looks like it's a location for the treasure.'

'Have you checked it out?' asked Mclean.

'Give us a few days,' said Capel. 'We are getting married tomorrow.'

'Touché,' said Mclean. 'You two relax while you can. I look forward to seeing you tomorrow.'

'Wow,' said Capel after hanging up, 'he was in a good mood. Probably down to his visitor.'

Before Vicky could reply the timer on her phone started to beep. 'Dinner's ready,' she said.'

It was only after the Christmas pudding that Capel's mind came back to the phone call. 'So what do you think this means about Russell Levine?'

Vicky sipped her glass of port. 'Assuming Roland's right, and he usually is, it looks like Levine wasn't the killer. Okay, it's possible he murdered Margaret and Cherie Taylor, but someone else killed him. Only it seems far more likely that by disposing of Levine, the original murderer was trying to make it look like as if Levine had done a runner and so put him in the frame. The only trouble is, we've run out of suspects.'

'So, what does our killer look like?'

'Sorry? If I knew that…'

'Don't be obtuse,' said Capel, waving an after-dinner mint in Vicky's direction. 'Let's go back to the beginning. He or she had to be in Marlborough on the night Margaret was killed and in Melksham when Cherie Taylor died. We're looking for someone who's an expert shot with a crossbow – it was an impressive feat, hitting someone on that moving ride – and it's also someone who had access to high tech equipment to produce the electromagnetic pulse that stopped the pacemaker.'

'Okay,' said Vicky. 'And they also needed access to dry ice and to a shotgun – though the gun's not that difficult in a country area. And seemed to be keeping pretty well on top of the investigation. Russell Levine was the perfect person to disappear and raise our suspicions at that stage of the investigation.'

'It's not likely to have been your mate Yaxley, then,' said Capel. 'He never seemed on top of anything.'

'I'm talking about the murderer, not the investigation,' said Vicky. 'Shit, Yaxley.'

'Oh, come on, it's obvious he wouldn't have the brains for this kind of thing.'

'Is there a type of biathlon where they use crossbows instead of guns?'

'Erm, have we lost the plot here?'

'Bear with me,' said Vicky.

'Okay, not that I'm aware of,' said Capel. 'Hang on.' He picked up his phone and typed into the browser. 'Almost. There's ski archery, but that's using a conventional bow... hang on. Yes, it's quite new. Not a recognised discipline yet, but apparently it's catching on fast. A mix of cross-country skiing and crossbow shooting. Why?'

'Jamie Sutton.'

'Sorry, wondercop?'

'Himself. According to Yaxley, Jamie is into some kind of biathlon that doesn't involve guns. And Yaxley said that Jamie claimed to have been seconded to the intelligence services...'

'... where according to Ed, you might get access to the electromagnetic pulse devices that don't officially exist. One of which went missing a few years ago.'

'Precisely. Jamie claimed he wasn't in Marlborough on the night of the Mop – but he volunteered to check the CCTV. So we don't know that's the case. Oh, yes, and guess who led the search of Russell Levine's house where the post-it with the late Ms Taylor's address on was found.'

'Sutton. Whoa – didn't someone say something about Margaret running for Police and Crime Commissioner? It was call-me-Suki, wasn't it? She said Margaret was going to run on rooting out police corruption...'

'And though we don't have any dirt on Jamie, it adds to the motive to get Miss LeVine out of the way if he was in the firing line.'

'So, what now? We can't go steaming in – this is all dependent on Russell Levine not having shot himself and Roland wasn't definitive about that. And we don't know about the CCTV or when – or even if – Sutton was really seconded to the security services. It could just have been showing off. Also, it is Christmas Day.

And we do have quite a full calendar tomorrow.'

'I can't argue with that. But between the wedding and the honeymoon, I need to talk to the Inspector. No, to Roland and then to the Inspector.'

'Will you be able to put this out your mind? I don't want it spoiling things?'

'Put what out of my mind? Speaking of which, when did you say Ed's turning up?'

'Late evening. He wanted to put the girls to bed before he came over.'

'Fine,' said Vicky, 'I just wanted to make sure I'd be out of here before he arrived.'

CHAPTER 19

The forecast had been for a clear day and Capel woke before his alarm to a clear sunrise. There was a crisp frost on the vicarage lawn. Boxing Day. Wedding day. He looked at himself in the mirror and grinned an idiotic grin. Pulling on a dressing gown, he knocked on the spare room door. 'Ed? Are you awake? Coffee?'

'Coffee in bed?' Unlike Capel, Ed was one of those irritating people who were immediately awake and alert. 'Best man's perks? I'll come down for breakfast.'

'Why not?' It seemed not quite real, as if Capel were acting in a play, as he wandered around the cold vicarage – the heating was on, but it was yet to make much of a mark on the freezing overnight temperatures – getting the coffee and then fixing breakfast for the two of them.

'Any doubts?' asked Ed, waving a piece of toast with a thick layer of marmalade at Capel. 'It's not too late to change your mind, you know. Better now than after the event.'

'No,' said Capel. 'Well, of course I have doubts in the sense that this is a huge undertaking, and no one can know the future. But I have no intention of changing my mind. Whose side are you on, anyway?'

'Yours,' said Ed. 'You seem to have forgotten, but it's what you said to me before I married Fliss, when you were still a carefree bachelor. I've never forgotten. Better to get it right now than to have a long and difficult disaster. Not that I think you will, any more than Fliss and I have.'

'Best to stop digging,' said Capel. 'And while I

think of it, no mucking about pretending that you've lost the rings. When you have married as many people as I have, the joke begins to wear thin.'

'Ah, yes, I'd forgotten you were a serial marrier.'

'Is there such a word? I actually really enjoy taking wedding services, but you do see some remarkable things. We had one wedding where they really did lose the ring and the best man came up with a ring pull off a can of lager as a substitute. Thankfully, we were able to borrow a more acceptable one from a member of the congregation.'

Ed snorted. 'I assure you, it will all go smoothly. In fact, once we've had breakfast, I'm nipping over to the prospective bride's place to make sure there are no hitches from that end. Except the one that you are going to get.'

Capel raised an eyebrow.

'Hitches. Getting hitched.'

'Yes,' said Capel, 'I got it. I just wasn't sure I wanted it. Are you coming back here to get dressed?'

'Too right, I'm not going to risk spilling champagne on my best suit. I think you were right, by the way, avoiding the whole morning suit thing. It always looks so stiff and formal. As far as my attire goes, this is just like an ordinary working day, but with better food. I suppose it is for you too, seeing as how it'll be in your place of work. Incidentally, when's the bishop turning up?'

'She's going to meet us in the church an hour before.'

'Excellent. I'll leave you in peace. Just don't get distracted and forget what you've got planned.'

~

Vicky was sipping a glass of champagne trying to get ready, although her phone rang every five minutes. She was just putting it down from her Auntie Lucy when it rang again in her hand. It was Jamie Sutton. She carefully put the glass down, giving herself time to decide whether or not to talk to him. After all, the thought that he could be a killer was just a theory. They didn't have all the evidence yet. She hit the green icon. 'Hi Jamie, I'm a bit busy right now.'

'Oh, of course – I'm sorry, I totally forgot. It's today you're making me a sad, lonely man, isn't it?'

'Piss off,' said Vicky. 'Seriously, I am busy. Is it urgent?'

'Nothing that can't wait. I just wanted to wish you the best with Capel… what was his first name? Norman?'

'Stephen!'

'Of course. Are you planning to vow to obey him?'

'Are you kidding? Do you think I ever do what he says? In his dreams.'

'Fair enough. I'll leave you to it. There's nothing I can do to help?'

'I'll be honest, if you really want to help me, you'll get off the line. Sorry, that's the champagne talking. But even if you're working on a mass murder, I need to go.'

'I understand. Have a great day.'

~

Capel pottered around the house, putting off getting ready. Nearly an hour after Ed left, the landline phone rang. Assuming it was Ed, Capel answered 'What have you forgotten?'

'Is that Mr Capel?' the voice was male, unfamiliar.

'Yes.'

'I'm Detective Constable Sutton. A colleague of Vicky's.'

The conversation with Vicky whirled through Capel's mind. 'Ah, yes, Jamie. She's not here, I'm afraid. I don't know if you know, but it's our wedding day.'

Sutton's voice hesitated for a moment. 'Yes, of course. I need your help. Could you bring the leather notebook that was taken from Margaret LeVine's house to the Combe Down Tunnel? You really shouldn't have taken evidence away.'

'Obviously not today,' said Capel. 'If it would be helpful, we're not actually going on honeymoon until the week after next. I could meet you later in the week.' Possibly with police backup.

'Sorry,' said Sutton. 'I need you to bring it now.'

'And I'm sorry too,' said Capel, 'but surely you can see that's not possible. Did you hear what I said? Vicky and I are getting married in a couple of hours.'

'I know that,' said Sutton. 'And I would very much like your celebrations to go ahead, which is why I need the notebook brought here, now. If you'd left it at LeVine's it would have been a whole lot simpler. I didn't realise its significance during the initial search.'

'I really don't get this,' said Capel. 'What's the urgency? There's nothing in the notebook that's relevant to Margaret's death. That's the only reason it's not still in evidence.'

'I don't think you are right,' said Sutton. 'Please don't make me insist.'

Capel pointlessly shook his head. 'Again, it's not

going to happen.' He restrained himself from biting at the flesh of his left hand between thumb and forefinger. Their suspicions about Jamie Sutton had solidified. He could feel the hairs prickling on the back of his neck.

'There's someone wants to speak to you,' said Sutton. Capel heard a scuffling, then Vicky's voice: 'Do what he says. Help me, Stephen!'

'Vicky?'

'I'm sorry,' said Sutton. 'She can't come to the phone again right now. I expect you here within 30 minutes, with the leather notebook. Please don't call anyone. Both your landline and your mobile are being monitored. I will know if you do make a call, and we don't want anything unpleasant to happen here. There's been enough unpleasantness already.' He hung up.

Capel stared around desperately. He didn't know if Sutton really could monitor his phone, but he wasn't taking any chances. There was something not right about the call. Vicky was clearly trying to tell him something – she never called him Stephen. She'd sounded strange too, but under the circumstances, it wasn't surprising. He picked up his laptop, then put it down again. If Sutton was monitoring his phones, he might also monitor emails. He opened the laptop again and logged into the most obscure email address he had – a free university alumni one – and started to type.

Hi, Ed. I hope all the preparations are going well and see you soon. I'm good. Just checking the music for the service – we're starting with the Tallis anthem Combe Descendit Ciniculum. It's a bit like the thing we did at West Kennet, so needs a very careful performance. Stephen x

He just hoped his Latin was holding up and that Ed wouldn't dismiss this as a joke of some sort. The reference to West Kennet, where Ed had nearly died a year before, would surely make it clear that this was not just a bit of fun.

The taxi, which was his only working car, took three goes to start. He started down the narrow, curving Summer Lane through the crisp morning air. The sun was out, but it was still below freezing and he took the bends carefully on the ungritted road. Where the lane crossed the Two Tunnels footpath, he tucked the taxi into a small layby and started to jog down the footpath towards the tunnel's north entrance.

~

'I'd better get back and make sure Capel's got his act together,' shouted Ed to Vicky's closed bedroom door.

'Hang on a minute,' said Vicky. A moment later the door opened and she stepped out in her wedding dress. Cream, stylish but simple, it looked, Ed thought, perfect for her.

'You'll knock 'em in the aisles, kid.'

'Ed, I know we haven't always seen eye to eye...'

'No need to say anything. I couldn't be happier for the two of you.' His phone buzzed and he glanced at it. 'Hang on, there's an email that appears to be from himself, though I don't recognise the address.'

'As soon as you get back you should be heading to the church.'

Ed pointed down at his jeans. 'I think I might need to change first.' He frowned and flicked up Google Translate on his phone. 'Okay, I don't want to worry you, but I think we've got a problem.'

~

The North gate to the tunnel had been shut, with a sign saying the tunnel was closed for the bank holiday, but the padlock on the gate was unlocked. Capel dragged the gate open and started to jog again. The tunnel was about a mile long, and though the lighting ran the whole length, it left everything in a mysterious twilight. The music wasn't playing this time, presumably because the tunnel was supposed to be closed. He reckoned he had been going for about three quarters of the length when he saw someone ahead, faint, but occluding the bright shape of the south entrance beyond.

Panting, Capel slowed to a walk, partly because his lungs felt about to burst, partly to be able to hear better.

'Mr Capel?' It was Jamie Sutton.

'Present.'

'I don't want any trouble.' Something glinted in Sutton's hand. As he drew nearer, Capel realised it was a handgun, an automatic.

'I've no intention of giving you any trouble. Where's Vicky?'

'In a minute. Give me your phone.'

Capel handed it over.

Sutton turned the phone off and dropped it on the floor. 'Thank you. And the notebook, please.'

Capel took the small leather book out of his pocket and handed it over.

'Thank you. I'm going to tie your hands behind your back and I want you to sit on the floor, okay?'

'Vicky?'

'Like I said, in a minute. She's safe, don't worry.' Sutton pulled Capel's hands together and fixed them with a cable tie round his wrists.

Capel slid down against the wall. 'What's this about?'

'We aren't having a conversation. I'll tell you when you need to contribute.'

'I need to know. Where's Vicky?'

'She's outside and she is safe. Concentrate on your own skin for now. Where does it tell you about the treasure?' He gestured at Capel with the notebook. 'I looked through it when I searched LeVine's house, but I didn't see anything relevant in there.'

'I will tell you,' said Capel, 'but first let me know why you did it, Jamie. What had Margaret LeVine or Cherie Taylor ever done to you? Surely it wasn't worth two lives to try to find some treasure that probably doesn't even exist.'

'LeVine was going to ruin my career. She'd been digging around when she was running for the Crime Commissioner job. She knew… stuff that couldn't come out. With Taylor, yes, it was about the treasure, because by then, who cared? I might as well go down for two as one. So, I get the idea it's got something to do with this notebook, but how do you read it?'

'There was a brooch.'

'I know. And there was a document about it in Cambridge that had some sort of code.'

'It was you, then. You called the university library? They rang Vicky and said a colleague of hers had rung.'

Sutton nodded. 'So, tell me all about it.' He cocked the gun and aimed at Capel. 'Now would be a good time to start.'

~

'What the hell are we going to do?' asked Vicky. 'Sorry, mum.' Her mother shrugged and poured out two glasses of champagne.

'He said he was going to Combe Down Tunnel,' said Ed, 'but I don't know if he's there yet. I'll see if we can find anything from his phone.'

'Will there be a signal if he's in the tunnel?'

'Yes, I think it's too shallow to cut things off entirely. Hang on…'

Vicky stared at the glass her mother had handed to her as if she didn't understand what it was.

'The phone's switched off,' Ed said.

'Oh, great,' said Vicky. 'The idiot.'

'He might not have had any choice. Anyway, it's probably the best thing. Whoever's with him is going to think we can't get a location from it because of that.'

'Maybe that's because it's switched off,' Vicky said, as if speaking to a child.

'The thing is,' said Ed, tapping on his phone as he spoke, 'people get the wrong idea about phones. It's not like switching off a light switch. There has to be some of its circuitry live so that when you hold in the on-switch it reboots the operating system. But the thing is, Capel asked me to put some monitoring software on his phone. He said he was always losing it. And he opted for the GHCQ special with the full bells and whistles.'

'Which means?'

'That we can do pretty much anything we like with his phone, including monitoring any conversations its microphones can pick up, without it appearing to be being switched on. Here we go, we're in.'

They listened in silence to the conversation between Capel and Sutton.

'Can I speak, or will he hear me?' Vicky whispered.

'It's not two way. Do you know who that is with Capel?'

Vicky nodded. 'My colleague from Marlborough, Detective Constable Jamie Sutton. Who we were beginning to think might be behind the murders. Where are they?'

'In the tunnel, about two hundred metres from the south entrance. I'm going to go and help Capel out.'

'No, *we're* going.'

'Vicky, I'm the best man. It's my job to make sure he gets to the church.'

'With due respect, Ed, fuck off. Sorry mum.' Vicky's mother, who had been following their conversation like a tennis match audience, shrugged again. 'We are both going. I'll take one end of the tunnel, you take the other.' Vicky pushed past Ed and opened the door. 'Are you coming?'

'You're going like that?' asked Ed, pointing to her wedding dress.

'Like you said, we're going to get him to the church. I won't have time to change twice.'

'Okay, but have you something dark you can wear over it? You'll stand out like a ghost in the tunnel with that on.'

'I've just the thing,' said Vicky. 'I borrowed it from Capel to get to the church if it was raining.' She pulled a full-length black cloak from the hall coat hooks and led the way to the car park.

'Okay,' said Ed, 'do you know how to get to the north entrance, the one off the lane from Capel's house?'

'Yes, sure. That's where we went last time.'

'It's best if we go separately. You go in that way, I'll take the south entrance. It sounded as if Sutton has a weapon. Do you have anything with you?'

'Just a baton in the car.'

'Okay, just a minute.' Ed opened the boot of his Jaguar and took out a holstered taser. 'Take this. Are you familiar with them?'

'Yes, of course. I won't ask why you've got it. But what about you?'

'I'm fine,' said Ed. 'After you. As soon as you get to the tunnel entrance, call me. We need to keep in touch.'

'Be careful.'

'I did learn a few things at West Kennet. Don't go into the tunnel until we're in contact. We've got to time this right.'

Ed watched Vicky set off, then pulled the Jaguar out behind her and followed closely. They drove around the outskirts of Bath from Vicky's mum's flat and through Thornton Down, passing the vicarage and the church, where there were already a few cars parked. Just outside the village, as Vicky's Golf roared along Summer Lane, Ed turned down onto the equally narrow Tucking Mill Lane. His electric car was near soundless as it hurtled along. He just hoped he wouldn't meet anyone out on an early Boxing Day walk. In places, the lane was so narrow his wing mirrors were brushing the hedges on both sides.

Just before a sharp bend, he came to a high wooden fence on the right with a sign for Tucking Mill reservoir, leading to a track through the trees. There was a wooden gate across the track. Ed jumped out of the car and peered at a sign saying the gate was automated. He pressed the button alongside it. The gate did not move. He put his shoulder against the gate and pushed. Still nothing. Muttering to himself, Ed ran back to the car and pressed down on the accelerator.

He was not going more than 10 miles per hour when he hit the gate, but it felt a lot faster. The heavy car juddered for a brief moment, then there was a loud bang and the gate flew open. Ed was half conscious of someone shouting from the garden of the house alongside. He slammed his foot down and shot up the track. It ended in a small, rough car park, in sight of the south entrance to the tunnel.

Vicky saw Capel's taxi as she turned a bend in the lane and pulled in behind it. Checking the taser was ready to use, she hauled up the cloak and her dress and sprinted down towards the tunnel entrance. As she got near, she drew out her phone and called Ed.

'Yes.'

'I'm nearly at the entrance. There's a gate across the tunnel.'

'Okay. Can you open it?'

'Yes, someone's unlocked it.'

Ed checked the location of Capel's phone. 'They're moving towards my end of the tunnel, about 150 metres north of me at the moment. So they're a lot closer to me than you. You need to get down your part of the tunnel as quickly as possible. If you can get a clear shot, taser the guy as soon as you can.'

'It's a straight tunnel,' said Vicky. 'He's going to see me.'

'Like I said, they're heading this way, so for the moment you'll be behind him. And there's a gradient, so you probably won't be visible initially. You need to get well oriented, moving steadily. Tell me when you have this end of the tunnel clearly visible and a few seconds after that the lights will go out. It's still vaguely possible you'll be visible against the north end of the tunnel, but I'm hoping there will be enough of a distraction from my end there won't be a problem.'

'Don't do anything stupid, right Ed?'

'Me, stupid? As if. Are you ready?'

'Yes.'

'Okay, start to jog down the tunnel. The lights should go off in about half a minute.'

CHAPTER 20

'So there was no point having the notebook?' Sutton waved the gun at Capel.

'Not once the code had been broken, no. Look, I'm not an action hero. Is there any chance of not pointing that thing at me? I'm sure you don't want an accident any more than I do.'

Sutton looked at the gun as if it was something strange he had found on the floor and slipped it into his belt. 'Did you find this rose marking?'

'I've been busy,' said Capel. 'We only found this out on Christmas Eve. My wedding today was higher up my priority list.'

'Let's take a look.' Sutton indicated with his head. 'Up. We're going walkies. I'd say we need to head about half way from here to the south entrance, then start searching.' He picked up a black holdall from the floor and pushed Capel to start walking ahead of him.

'What are you trying to do here?' Capel asked. 'Even if we find the rose, it's likely to take days to excavate anything buried there. And if you could get your hands on the treasure, you'll still be wanted for murder. They will work out it's you after this, whether or not I survive. The best option is just to give yourself up.'

'You forget, Capel, I'm police. I know that "best to give yourself up" crap is just a line to encourage people to confess. We give this a couple of hours and if we don't find anything, I'm leaving the country anyway. But if I can do it with some treasure tucked away, so much the better.'

'They'll miss me before then. I'm supposed to be

getting married, remember. In under an hour.'

'They'll miss you, sure. But that's very different from finding out where we are. If you're helpful I'll turn on your phone so they can track you down as I'm leaving. If not… whether they find you or not won't make much difference.' Sutton pointed to the distances marked on the floor. 'We're 100 metres from the entrance, which I reckon is where we start looking.'

~

Ed jogged up to the south tunnel gates, but he could see even before he was there that this end was locked. 'Damnation.' It was a sturdy padlock and he had nothing in the car that could cut through it. He pulled a small leather pouch out of his jacket pocket and extracted a couple of lock picks. 'It's like riding a bike,' he muttered to himself. 'You never forget.'

Vicky stopped for a moment to catch her breath, leaning against the damp-feeling bricks of the tunnel wall. She could now see the far end of the tunnel as a spot of brightness that had been hidden before by the internal lighting. The last distance marker she had passed said she was 500 metres from the south entrance. But the light was too dim to make out Capel and Sutton. She was going to have to tread lightly from now on. And it was surely more than thirty seconds since Ed's call. Maybe something had gone wrong. It wasn't going to stop her, but she would rather not do this on her own. She pulled at the long black cloak, making sure it was covering as much of her dress as possible and started to jog again.

'Bloody idiot,' Ed commented to himself as he

dropped one of the lock picks. He scrabbled to pick it up and tried again. There was a click and the padlock popped open. Ed stuck the lock and the picks in his pocket and sent a text to a government location he had contacted on his car journey. In a movie there would have been the thud of a circuit breaker for dramatic effect, but the string of lights down the tunnel he could see through the bars of the gate suddenly went silently off, leaving the tunnel in darkness. He gave it a few seconds, hoping that by now Sutton would be focused on getting a light, rather than checking the entranceway, and eased open the gate, loping soundless down the edge of the path so he would not be silhouetted against the light.

~

'Shit! Stop where you are.' It took a moment for Sutton to get straight in his head what had just happened. He scrambled his phone out of his pocket.

Capel struggled to see what was going on. If he was going to do anything, surely now was the moment, but he couldn't be sure how easily Sutton could get the gun out. Within moments, Sutton had turned his phone's light on and shone it into Capel's eyes, leaving him virtually blinded.

'This isn't good,' said Sutton. 'Someone knows we're here.'

'Not necessarily,' said Capel, rubbing his eyes. 'It's Boxing Day, the tunnel's supposed to be closed. The lights could be set to go off anyway – it could be on a timer.'

Sutton put his hand over the phone's light and peered in both directions. To the north there was just the faintest spot of brightness without the lighting to wash it out. The south entrance, 100 metres away was much clearer. For a moment he thought he saw movement, but the trees outside the entrance were blowing in the wind, and surely that was what had caught his eye. He scanned the brickwork on either side with the narrow beam of light. 'One pace at a time and we look out for the rose. If you spot it, tell me.'

'Surely there's no time to do anything now, if you're right and someone knows we're here.'

'We just have to make time, don't we?'

It was hard to make out what Sutton was doing, but Capel caught a glint of light as Sutton took the gun from his belt.

'I'll try to spot it,' said Capel. 'But I can hardly see anything. You blinded me when the lights went out.'

Sutton shrugged and started to pace down the tunnel, one step at a time, sweeping the brickwork either side.

'Wait.' Capel knelt down by the left-hand tunnel wall. 'Shine it here.'

Sutton backed up and rested the side of the gun on Capel's back. 'What is it?'

Capel took a tissue from his pocket and wiped the surface of one of the yellowish bricks. It was at the end of a brickwork section: the next part of the wall was rougher, as if it were hewn out of rock. Incised on the surface of the brick was a stylised rose.

'Well spotted,' said Sutton. He unzipped his holdall with the hand that was holding the gun and took out a crowbar. 'I'm going to give this to you, and you are going to try to get that brick out. Please don't think that a crowbar makes a good weapon, because

I'm going to stand back with the gun trained on you. Any sudden movements and I won't hesitate to shoot. Do you understand?'

'Yes.'

Sutton threw the crowbar onto the paved surface, where it bounced painfully off Capel's right foot, and took a couple of steps back towards the opposite wall of the tunnel. 'Go on then. Shift it.'

Ed was now close enough to hear Sutton. Looking beyond Sutton and Capel up into the darkness of the tunnel, he caught sight of a shifting glimmer, like a white aurora. Vicky's dress couldn't be covered well enough. Sutton had only to look that way and he would see her. Ed couldn't see exactly where the gun was pointed, but if Sutton caught sight of Vicky he was likely to shoot before Ed could do anything. Ed had a gun himself, but any attempt to shoot Sutton was just as likely to hit Capel or Vicky. He couldn't risk it.

Capel wedged the crowbar between the brick and the rock and heaved. The brick shifted slightly.

'Put your back into it,' said Sutton.

Ed thought – hoped – that Vicky was now close enough to deploy the taser. He took a deep breath, yelled 'Now!' and threw himself to the floor as close as he could to the wall of the tunnel, so he was least likely to be visible.

Sutton turned and fired his gun towards the south entrance, the sound horribly loud in the confined space. He pointed the gun towards the ground and fired again, raising a yelp of pain from Ed, then swivelled back to look in the other direction, pushing the hot muzzle of the gun at Capel's head and using his other hand to show Capel in its light. 'You! Up the tunnel! I can see you moving. Walk slow towards me keeping your arms by your side. Any sudden movements and he gets it.'

Vicky pulled the cloak closer around her and started walking steadily towards Sutton. The cloak only fastened at her breast. She held it with one hand, bringing the taser up underneath it at waist level. 'Jamie, it's me. Are you okay, Capel?'

Keeping the gun at Capel's temple, Sutton swung the light around towards Vicky.

'I'm not hurt,' said Capel.

'Shut it,' said Sutton. 'Oh, Vicky, what a way to spend your wedding day. Look, you don't need to get hurt. No one does, except the guy on the floor back there. Keep coming until you're a couple of metres away then turn round so I can fix your hands behind your back.'

Vicky was half blinded by the phone's light. She could no longer make out Ed on the floor the other side of Sutton. 'Put the gun down, Jamie. It's over. Backup'll be here any minute. You know how this ends.'

Sutton shook his head. 'I'll secure you and leg it. I don't think you've got backup.'

Lying on the tunnel floor, Ed tried to make out Sutton in the gloom. The only figure he could see clearly was Vicky, illuminated by Sutton's light. He still couldn't get a safe shot at Sutton and in seconds Vicky would be near enough for Sutton to grab her. There was only one hope he could see, and it relied on Vicky picking up on his lead. Wincing from a pain in his forehead, he turned his gun to face away from the others, down towards the south tunnel opening, and fired.

As the shot rang out, Sutton swung the light back towards Ed, taking the gun away from Capel's head. Vicky stopped dead, pushed the taser through the gap in the cloak and pulled the trigger. There was a sharp crack and Sutton started to twitch, dropping the gun and his phone. The light went out, leaving them in darkness apart from the glow from the end of the tunnel. Vicky heard Sutton drop to the floor as his silhouette disappeared. She dropped the taser and pulled a torch from the cloak's inner pocket, lighting the unconscious Sutton. 'It's me. Capel, are you okay? Ed?'

Capel eased up, back to the tunnel wall, still holding the crowbar. 'I'm fine. Did you say Ed?' He turned towards the south entrance, where Ed was trying to stand.

'She did,' said Ed from behind them. 'Ouch.' He rubbed at his forehead. 'I think I must have got hit by a chip from the flooring the second time he fired. Have you any handcuffs?'

'Oddly enough, no. Not in my wedding dress,' said Vicky, hurrying over to Capel.

'There are cable ties in the bag,' said Capel.

Vicky fixed Sutton's hands behind his back, then shone her torch onto Ed. Blood was streaming down his forehead. 'Are you sure you're all right, Ed? That looks bad.'

'Nothing a paracetamol won't cure,' said Ed. 'Scalp wounds always look worse than they really are.' He pulled out his phone and called the police.

Vicky hugged Capel. 'Shit, you had me scared then.'

'Sorry,' said Capel. 'Next time I get married, I'll try not to be kidnapped on the day.'

'Idiot. What was he thinking? Sutton, I mean?'

'I don't know that he was thinking clearly. He hoped to get his hands on some treasure, any treasure and then to get out of the country. He didn't say where.'

Ed put his phone away and came over. 'They should be here in about 15 minutes. I've called your boss, Vicky, and explained. Chief Inspector Morley's going to keep the wedding guests busy and said she'd make sure your colleagues don't detain us longer than needs be, though we'll have to go the station between the service and the reception to give statements.'

~

Capel looked at Ed as they stood side by side in front of the chancel step of St Swithun's, Thornton Down. His best man had a dark stain on his shirt, but they had managed to clean up his face and stemmed the flow of blood.

'I should have known that being your best man wouldn't be easy,' said Ed. 'At least no one blew me up this time.'

'Up yours, Ridge,' said Capel.

Bishop Emma, standing in front of them, raised an eyebrow. 'Are you sure you're okay to go ahead with this? It'd be entirely understandable if you wanted to postpone.'

Capel shook his head. 'Vicky and I are certain.'

The bishop nodded to the organist. 'It looks like we're ready to go, then.'

Capel glanced back to see Vicky, still wearing the cloak over her dress, standing next to her mother at the back of the church. The organist began the processional music, Purcell's Trumpet Tune. Capel looked up at the cross on the altar and tried to focus his mind. He felt, rather than saw, Vicky arrive at his side and turned to face her. Somewhere along the way up the aisle she had taken off the cloak. Her dress was pristine, undamaged, though he had to suppress a smile when he noticed she had not had a chance to change into her wedding shoes and still wore her Doc Marten's underneath.

The bishop cleared her throat. 'God is love, and those who live in love live in God: and God lives in them. We have come together in the presence of God to witness the marriage of Stephen and Victoria, to ask his blessing on them, and to share in their Joy…'

~

Two days later, Ed rang the bell at the Vicarage. Vicky answered the door. 'Good afternoon, Detective Constable Capel,' Ed said.

'Actually, I'm sticking with Denning as my professional name,' said Vicky. 'Mrs Capel is the vicar's wife, but it's still DC Denning at work.'

'Good compromise,' said Ed.

'Come on in, Capel's in the kitchen.'

'How was the hotel?' Ed asked as he followed Vicky down the hall.

'Brilliant. I've always loved Castle Combe and the Manor was a wonderful place to stay. Thanks for fixing it up. It made it special.'

'You don't mind not going straight off on the honeymoon?'

'It makes it better,' said Capel as the others came into the kitchen. 'It makes it more of a celebration if we've time to appreciate being married before we head off.'

'I just thought you'd like to be brought up to date,' said Ed.

'What I don't get,' said Vicky, 'is why that dramatic murder of poor Margaret LeVine in the first place. It surely made it more likely that Jamie… that Sutton would be found out.'

Ed shrugged and took a coffee that Capel offered him. 'It seems that Sutton was both a fantasist and something of a show-off. He wanted his work to be admired as special. It seems he'd been on the make for months. Once Margaret LeVine forced him into a corner, he planned it all like it was a show. Starring him.'

'How did he get hold of the liquid nitrogen?' asked Capel.

'Apparently he had researched it all and he was prepared to order some from a catering supplier to a fake restaurant address. But as it happened there was a flask of liquid nitrogen in the evidence room at Marlborough from another case. He was like a magpie, collecting things that might be useful. That's how he got the EMP device he used on Cherie Taylor. His story of being seconded to the security services wasn't entirely inaccurate. He did spend a few months with MI5 before they decided he was totally unsuitable. My contact there has totally denied that they have such a device, and even if they did have that Sutton could not have stolen one, so that's definitely how he got it.'

'Any news of the treasure?' asked Vicky.

Ed shook his head. 'We've had ground penetrating radar in and there doesn't seem to be anything there.

Either they took out everything at the time the brooch was found and your churchwarden squirreled the rest away somewhere, or there was never anything other than the brooch. Let's face it, this wasn't a well-documented site.'

'So it's not going to be excavated?' said Capel.

'No – which is just as well. If you'd managed to get that brick out, it's entirely possible it would have caused a minor cave-in. They've shut the tunnel for now until the wall can be reinforced.'

Vicky shuddered. 'I've no sympathy for him, but I don't envy Sutton. They don't treat coppers well in prison. Even so, he deserves everything he gets.'

Ed raised his mug as if he were toasting them. 'Don't make this about him. I'll say it again: here's to the two of you. It couldn't have happened to a nicer couple.'

Capel looked across at Vicky. 'Thanks, Ed. One thing's for certain. Vicky and I won't forget our wedding day.'

Vicky smiled back at Capel. 'I'd hope you wouldn't anyway.' She took a drink of coffee. 'So, who is up for a walk? It's really sunny out there.'

'As long as there are no tunnels involved,' said Capel, 'that's a great idea.'

HISTORICAL NOTE

The Anglo-Saxon Chronicle is a real thing – a fascinating mix of history, gossip and fake news written by monks, covering dates ranging from 1 to 1154 AD – later entries were added year by year, and so are far more detailed, while the earlier entries were looking back in history even when the Chronicle was first written. There are seven extant manuscripts, sometimes paralleling each other well and at other times showing marked divergence.

The very first entry in the Chronicle (apart from some background on Britain), for the year 1 reads (in translation – not entirely surprisingly, the original was in Anglo-Saxon – and with some variation between sources on the number of years) 'Octavian reigned 66 years and in the 52nd year of his reign Christ was born.'

The quotes from the Chronicle used in the novel are accurate, except for the phrase about the various and privy treasures of the reeve Alfred, which was added for the benefit of the story. Ethelred was the English king landed with the unfortunate-sounding nickname 'the unready' – not because he was unready for the invasion led by Swein Forkbeard (a name worthy of Tolkien, who was, of course, an expert on the period), but because he was ill-advised (unræd in Anglo-Saxon), which was both true and a play on his name, which meant well-advised. Swein became king in 1013, but died the next year and Ethelred was restored to the throne for two years, when he was succeeded on his death by Swein's son, Cnut, a.k.a. King Canute of holding back the tide fame.

The quotes used are taken from *The Anglo-Saxon Chronicle, a revised translation*, edited by Dorothy Whitelock (Eyre and Spottiswoode, 1961).

Words of the Marriage Service are from *The Alternative Service Book* (Cambridge University Press, 1980).

Being Lancastrian, I have used the opportunity to bring in some Northern colour by playing fast and loose with the location of a number of legends and traditions. Both the legends mentioned in the book and the Pace Egg play that surprises Capel are historically accurate, but they are Lancashire traditions, rather than from the Bath area.

Dildrum originates in South Lancashire, while the Pace Egg play was common across the county. Apologies to Somerset locals, but I couldn't resist bringing in stories and a play that I had experienced in my youth.

ABOUT THE AUTHOR

Brian Clegg is a prize-winning popular science writer. His most recent books are *What Do You Think You Are?* and the puzzle-solving book *Conundrum*, with over 30 other popular science titles including *Inflight Science, Before the Big Bang,* and *How to Build a Time Machine*. His *Dice World* and *A Brief History of Infinity* were both longlisted for the Royal Society Prize for Science Books.

Born in Rochdale, Lancashire, Brian read Natural Sciences (specializing in experimental physics) at Cambridge University. After graduating, he spent a year at Lancaster University where he gained a second MA in Operational Research.

From Lancaster, he joined British Airways, where he formed a new department tasked with developing hi-tech solutions for the airline. His emphasis on innovation led to training with creativity guru Dr Edward de Bono, and in 1994 he left BA to set up his own creativity consultancy.

Brian has written regular columns, features and reviews for numerous magazines and newspapers, including The Wall Street Journal, Nature, BBC Focus, Physics World, The Observer, Good Housekeeping and Playboy. His books have been translated into many languages, including German, French, Spanish, Portuguese, Chinese, Japanese, Polish, Norwegian, and Indonesian.

Brian has given sell-out lectures at the Royal Institution, the British Library and the Science Museum and many other venues. He has also contributed to radio and TV programs, and is a popular speaker at schools. Brian is editor of the successful popularscience.co.uk book review site and blogs at brianclegg.blogspot.com. Brian lives in Wiltshire with his wife and twin daughters. In his spare time, he has a passion for Tudor and Elizabethan church music.

A FAIR DELIVERANCE

OTHER TITLES BY BRIAN CLEGG

FICTION

A Lonely Height (A Stephen Capel novel)
A Timely Confession (A Stephen Capel novel)
A Spotless Rose (A Stephen Capel novel)
A Twisted Harmony (A Stephen Capel novel)
An End to Innocence (A Stephen Capel novel)
A Fall from Grace (A Stephen Capel novel)

Conundrum – 100 puzzles and code-breaking challenges

Oberland

Organizing a Murder (Murder Mystery Party Games)

Xenostorm: Rising

A FAIR DELIVERANCE

NON-FICTION

What Do You Think You Are?
Scientifica Historica
Dark Matter and Dark Energy
Everyday Chaos
Professor Maxwell's Duplicitous Demon
The Graphene Revolution
Gravitational Waves
The Reality Frame
Cracking Quantum Physics
Big Data
What Colour is the Sun?
Are Numbers Real?
How Many Moons Does the Earth Have?
Ten Billion Tomorrows
Science for Life
Final Frontier
The Quantum Age
Extra Sensory
Dice World
Gravity
Introducing Infinity
The Universe Inside You
How to Build a Time Machine
Inflight Science
Armageddon Science
Before the Big Bang
Ecologic
Upgrade Me
The Global Warming Survival Kit
The Man Who Stopped Time
The God Effect
A Brief History of Infinity
Roger Bacon: The First Scientist
Light Years

Printed in Great Britain
by Amazon